DANGER, 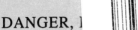

David Schutte v
Brain surgeon,
just some of the things he never achieved. He is now
a financial adviser and specialist children's book-
seller. He lives near Midhurst in West Sussex with his
wife and children.

Danger, Keep Out! is the first book in the Naitabal
Mystery series. It was previously published under the
title 'Mud Pies and Water-Bombs'. The other titles in
the series are *Wake Up, It's Midnight!*, *Wild Woods,
Dark Secret* and *Behind Locked Doors*.

Also by David Schutte

Wake Up, It's Midnight!
Wild Woods, Dark Secret
Behind Locked Doors

DAVID SCHUTTE

DANGER, KEEP OUT!

A Naitabal Mystery

To Jenny

Best wishes

David Schutte

MACMILLAN
CHILDREN'S BOOKS

First published 1993 by Pan Books Ltd
as *Mud Pies and Water-bombs*

This edition published 1996
by Macmillan Children's Books
a division of Macmillan Publishers Limited
25 Eccleston Place, London SW1W 9NF
and Basingstoke

Associated companies throughout the world

ISBN 0 330 34728 4

3 5 7 9 8 6 4 2

A CIP catalogue record for this book is available from
the British Library

Phototypeset by Intype, London
Printed and bound in Great Britain by
Mackays of Chatham, PLC, Chatham, Kent

TO

Katy Schutte
Chief of all the Naitabals

WITH LOVE

NAITABAL:
A WILD SPECIES OF HUMAN, AGED ABOUT TEN.

Habitat: Found in most British gardens all the year round, sometimes as an unexpected visitor.

Nesting: Mainly in trees, often in a tree-house.

Feeding: Eats anything, except what its parents want it to.

Song: Loud (irritating to adults), with its own secret language.

Recognition: You'll know one when you've seen one.

THE NAITABAL EARTH SONG
(IN ENGLISH)

The Naitabal Tree
Spreads its branches
Over those who
Deserve to be there.

Only the good
Who look after
The Earth
Shall keep it.

(For a full rendering in Naitabal language, see Chapter 14)

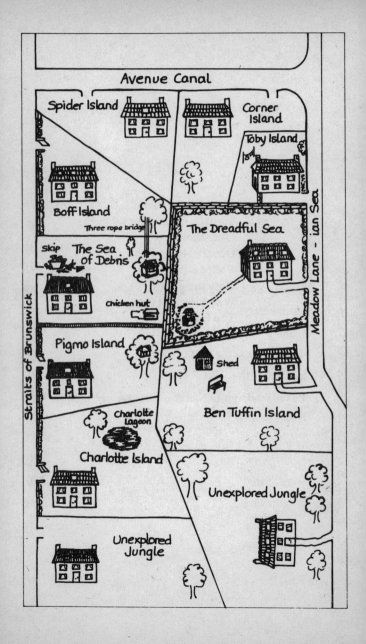

Contents

CHAPTER ONE

The Mysterious Sinking
of the SS *Coates*

Ben heard a noise and woke up. He was lying on the floor of the Naitabal tree-house, and the first thing he noticed was the lemonade bottle. It was shining like a ghost in the bright moonlight that spilled through the windows. And it was empty. It hadn't been empty before he went to sleep. He checked his watch. Midnight.

"You've drunk all the lemonade," he said accusingly into the half darkness.

There was no answer. He turned over and raised himself on one elbow. Toby, who was supposed to be on watch, lay on the floor in a not-very-watchful heap.

"You've drunk all the lemonade," Ben repeated, louder.

Toby's breath whistled in and out of his nose in peaceful slumber. An empty biscuit-wrapper just in front of it fluttered up and down in the breeze.

"And I see you've eaten all the biscuits as well," added Ben. "Now we've nothing left for breakfast."

Toby stopped nose-whistling and snuggled further down. His voice was muffled by several layers of sleeping bag.

"Sorry."

"And you were supposed to be on watch."

"The lemonade and biscuits made me sleepy."

"I'm not surprised. There was supposed to be enough for both of us."

"Well, I was bored. I couldn't stop."

"Thanks a lot."

"I offered you some, but you were asleep."

"Oh, great.'

"Don't worry," said Toby, yawning, "I'll go and get some more."

"It's midnight. You won't be able to get in."

Toby sat up slowly.

"Yes, I will. We never lock the house. Anyway, the window's jammed open. We use that."

"Aren't you afraid of burglars?"

"There's nothing to steal."

Ben thought of Toby's house and said, "No – I suppose not."

Toby climbed sleepily to his feet, then heaved himself up on the branch that ran at an angle through the middle of the tree-house. He opened the escape hatch in the roof and disappeared.

Ben stood up and watched through the north window. Toby made his way along the three-rope bridge to the oak on Boff Island. It was Boff's garden, really, but to the Naitabals it was Boff Island.

From the west window of the tree-house Ben could see Mr Elliott's garden, which they called the Sea of Debris. You had to cross the Sea to get to the other islands. It was funny how it looked neat and tidy in the moonlight. During the day it was a mess, filled with all sorts of timber, fireplaces, roofing tiles and other useless things that Mr Elliott had been throwing into it for forty years. But now it looked peaceful. No dust or rubbish to be seen, just a builder's garden painted silvery-blue by the moon.

Further to the left, Charlotte's house showed a single light in the hall downstairs. All the others were in darkness, quiet and still.

Then Ben heard a faint noise outside. Was it the Igmopong? They were the rival gang who had a tree-house in the next door garden. The Igmopong's tree-house was very inferior, and it was vital for the Naitabals to protect theirs from illegal occupation while the padlock on the roof was broken. It couldn't be replaced until tomorrow, and they couldn't take the risk of leaving it overnight.

He peered into the darkness. Something must have made the noise, and something must have woken him up, but he still couldn't see anything unusual.

He crept to the east side of the hut where Miss Coates's garden lay. Her garden was called the Dreadful Sea because Miss Coates was so dreadful to see. There had always been something odd about Miss Coates. The way she grew hedges all round her garden so that no one could see into it. How she went frantic if anyone dared to climb a tree in one of the surrounding gardens. And when Mr Elliott had built the tree-house for them in *his* garden – what a fuss! She had made quite sure that no windows overlooked *her* precious garden.

But who needed windows, thought Ben. He crouched down, rotated a little wooden cover, and put his eye to the hole that had been drilled underneath. Peep-holes were much more exciting.

It took a few moments for his eye to adjust to the scene. To his surprise, he saw her. The noise must have been her back door opening. The old enemy battleship, the SS *Coates*, was at large, steaming up the garden path with a torch. Her white hair glowed in the moonlight.

She stopped at the well in the middle of her lawn, and shone her torch into it. What happened next was so unbelievable that it took a lot of explaining to the other Naitabals in the morning.

"What do you mean, she disappeared?"

It was Charlotte who said it. She kept her voice low in case the Igmopong were listening.

13

The five Naitabals were sitting with their legs dangling out of the trap-door in the floor of the Naitabal hut, trying to hit each other's feet with Naitabal acorns. Except Boff, whose feet were motionless, but whose mind was working instead. Down below them, Mr Elliott's chickens clucked and scratched and fussed around in the corner enclosure in the Sea of Debris.

Charlotte was ten and pretty, but her mouth was too big, and her teeth didn't meet at the front. Much to the envy of the others, she was the only one who could suck a drink through six straws with her teeth clenched.

"She can't have just disappeared down the well!"

"*Well*, she did," said Ben, making a joke of it. His brown eyes and cheeky face were less bright than usual.

Charlotte looked at him closely.

"You look as if you didn't get much sleep."

"We didn't. We were up all night after that, both of us."

"Burke, burke, burke," said a chicken, as if to criticise them for being such idiots.

"Oh, shut up!" said Ben, and threw an acorn at it. He missed, and the hen clucked derisively.

"She can't have gone *right* into it," said Charlotte again. "Not *right in*! People don't go down wells."

"She *did*!" said Ben, hissing. "I saw her go *right in*. And when Toby came back with Coke and mince pies we *both* saw her come right out! Didn't we, Toby?"

"Yep," said Toby, droopy-eyed. He had a habit of falling asleep at the best of times, but being up all night was making it doubly difficult for him to function properly. He added lazily, "Perhaps she needed water and the rope broke and she went down the well to get the bucket back."

"Yes, Toby," said Ben. "Very likely."

Jayne, who hadn't spoken yet, was a new Naitabal and

not quite sure of her ground. She thought it safest to support Charlotte.

"But she can't have gone *down* the *well*!" she protested. She was like a beautiful little doll with her jet-black curly hair and trim, delicate figure, but her looks were deceptive. Underneath the beautiful smile she could be quite formidable when roused. "It's impossible! Old ladies don't do that sort of thing!"

"I think you both fell asleep and dreamed it," said Charlotte. "You're both half asleep now."

"Why don't you tell us *exactly* what happened?" suggested Jayne.

"I'm trying to, but everyone keeps saying it's impossible, and it can't be, and that we couldn't have seen it."

"We'll listen – promise."

Four of them stood up and checked the surrounding islands for any sign of the Igmopong. Then they dangled their legs again and resumed throwing acorns.

"It was midnight," said Ben, when he was sure everyone was listening. "There was a little bit of moonlight, but not much. When I looked through the porthole I saw the lights of a ship steaming up the Border Straits."

"He means a torch, coming up the path," Toby explained drowsily to Jayne. As a new Naitabal she hadn't yet learned the jargon.

"Was it the SS *Coates*?" asked Charlotte.

"Definitely. Her white hair – sorry, the steam from her funnel – always glows in the dark."

Boff raised his curly hair, bushy eyebrows and spectacles all at once and said, "Something she puts on it," and went back to his calculations.

"Probably radioactive and highly dangerous when she's just done her hair," said Toby.

"She doesn't put her head in a hairdryer," said Charlotte, "she puts it in a nuclear fallout shelter."

The others laughed.

"Poor Miss Coates," said Jayne.

"SS *Coates*," corrected Boff automatically, without looking up.

"Her hair looks a bit like a mushroom cloud, come to think of it," said Toby.

The jokes exhausted, all eyes turned again to Ben.

"What happened then?"

Ben waited until the cockerel down below them had finished doodling its "oo", or whatever cockerels do.

"The SS *Coates* turned off its lights and lay at anchor for a few minutes. Making sure there were no more ships around."

"But no one can see into her garden, anyway," protested Charlotte. "With all those trees and hedges and brick walls in the way. You can't even see into it from upstairs in your house, can you? And you're right next door."

"Well, anyway – that's what she did. She seemed to be fiddling with something. It looked as if she was winding the handle that brings up the bucket. And then" – Ben's eyes glowed with excitement as he recalled the next part – "then she switched her torch on again, lifted her leg over the wall of the well, and climbed into it! At first I thought she must have been standing in the bucket! But then she went lower and lower, the torchlight got fainter and fainter – and she was gone!"

There was a stunned and thoughtful silence. Then Charlotte said, "And then?"

"Nothing. Nothing happened at all until Toby came back with the mince pies and Coke."

"And you stopped watching and ate them all, I suppose?" – accusingly.

"No, we didn't! I told Toby what I'd seen, and he didn't believe it either – thought I'd made a mistake or couldn't see properly, or was going bonkers. Then we *both* looked out through the peepholes – sorry, portholes. Toby started saying he'd had enough, and it was all nonsense, and I must have been dreaming. Then he went to get a mince pie because he was starving, and just as he was swigging some Coke, she started surfacing again."

"We'll have to call her the Submarine *Coates* now," said Toby, beginning to wake up properly.

"*Did* you see, Toby?"

"Oh, yes, I saw," said Toby. "Ben was right. First there was a bit of light showing inside the well, then it got brighter, and then billows of white hair appeared and up she came."

"And what happened then?"

"Oh," said Toby, "she fiddled with buckets and ropes and things and then went back into her house."

"And that was all?"

"Yes."

They all thought in silence for a bit, then Jayne summed it up for all of them, "What a funny thing," she said, and Boff murmured, "I wonder what she was doing?"

"She's up to no good, that's for sure," said Ben. "My father thinks there's something fishy about her, anyway, because she's so secretive about her garden. He says she's been like it for over forty years – ever since her father died after the last war."

"Perhaps he's not dead," said Toby. "Perhaps he fell down the well and broke his legs and she has to go down and feed him."

"What – for forty years?" said Boff, looking up again.

"Miss Coates is over sixty," said Ben, "so her father would be about ninety by now."

"And it wouldn't take his legs *that* long to mend," protested Charlotte.

"It might," said Toby, clinging to his argument, "if they were broken badly enough and didn't" – he mouthed the words loftily – "receive proper medical attention."

"Anyway," said Boff, "the point is – what are we going to do about it?"

"The first thing is to have a look at the well," said Jayne.

"And see if *we* can go down it," said Charlotte.

"And see what's down there," said Jayne.

"Perhaps she goes down to see if there's any water left," suggested Toby.

"She could use the bucket for that."

"I wonder how deep it is?" said Charlotte, suddenly.

"It might just be orna – orna – mental," said Ben. "My grandfather says it's orna – mental 'cos he doesn't think there was a proper well there before the war and he can't see why she'd have a proper one dug today."

"If it's ornamental," said Boff, "how did she go down it?"

"Perhaps it's miles deep," said Toby.

"I wonder what would happen," said Ben, latching on to the idea, "if you dug a well so deep that it came out at the other side of the earth?"

"It would fill with sea water at the other end," said Toby, "and come through so fast there'd be a huge fountain in the sky. It would spray all the crops for years until England was just mud and paddy fields."

"No, it wouldn't," said Charlotte. "The middle of the earth is molten rock. So even if you *could* get a hole right through the middle, the water would come gushing out as a massive jet of steam. It would go right up to the clouds and make the greenhouse effect even worse."

"You couldn't *actually* have a hole, of course," said Boff. "Molten rock would fill it up every time you took the drill out."

"No, but just *supposing*," said Ben. "Engineers can do all sorts of things these days. They could put in a steel-lined tube or something, to keep the molten rock out of the way."

This idea was so absurd that Boff was speechless.

"*I* think," concluded Toby, "that all the oceans would dry up."

"Why?"

"Because all the water would be in the hole."

A bright chicken, as if disagreeing, said, "Burke, burke, burke," again.

Then Ben said, "Just suppose there *was* a hole right through the middle of the earth . . . and suppose it came out on *dry land* on the other side? What would happen if the SS *Coates* fell down the hole?"

"You'd never see her again," said Charlotte, briefly.

"Oh, good," said Ben.

"Unless you had a searchlight," said Toby.

"And a telescope," said Jayne, not to be outdone.

They laughed. Boff waited patiently to see what other ridiculous notions his fellow Naitabals could come up with.

"She'd shoot right through the earth and come out on the other side at thousands of miles an hour," said Ben. "She might go so fast she'd shoot right out into space," he added hopefully.

The corners of Boff's mouth started to twitch. He had had enough of their wild ideas.

"Oh-oh!" said Charlotte, reading his face. "Boff knows *exactly* what would happen. You can tell by the look."

"Well, to start with," said Boff, "she'd only go at a hundred and twenty miles an hour. It's the same as free-falling from an aeroplane."

They all imagined Miss Coates flying at a hundred and twenty miles an hour, her white hair blowing straight up and her dress billowing like a parachute.

Boff took out his always-handy calculator. "It would take nearly a day and a half just to reach the middle of the earth."

"Wow!"

"Just think of it! The SS *Coates* falling for a whole day and a half!"

"It could be a new sport."

"Mind you, it wouldn't be much fun – it'd be dark."

"Not if she took a torch."

"The batteries wouldn't last for a day and a half."

"She could take spares."

"I bet you couldn't change batteries at a hundred and twenty miles an hour," said Toby.

Charlotte was trying to imagine her falling out of the hole at the other end. "But what would happen after she got to the middle?"

"When you're right in the middle of the earth, gravity is cancelled out," said Boff. "So, as she fell past the middle, she'd slow down. Then she'd fall back towards the middle again."

"Oh, no!" came a chorus of voices.

"And she'd keep doing that until she came to a stop in the centre of the Earth. Then she'd be weightless *for ever.*"

Several Naitabal mouths fell open.

"I'd climb out again," said Ben.

"You wouldn't."

"I would."

"You *couldn't!*"

"I could!"

"OK, OK," said Boff firmly. "You probably could, but it would take you about forty years."

"Ha, ha!" said Toby, triumphant. "That's where Miss Coates's father is, then! Still climbing back up!"

Everyone seemed to have run out of ideas, and they returned to the problem of the well.

"When are we going to look at it?" said Charlotte.

Four eager faces looked to Ben for the answer, because Ben was fearless and adventurous. He was also the only one stupid enough to cross the Dreadful Sea in broad daylight.

"I'll look," he said. "This afternoon, when I come back from lunch."

They all contemplated the dangerous mission that Ben had volunteered to undertake, braving it alone against the SS *Coates*.

"And, as Jayne has only just joined us, we'll spend the afternoon teaching her Naitabal language."

"If you ever return," said Charlotte.

"I'll try," said Ben.

"Burke, burke, burke," said the chicken.

CHAPTER TWO

Across the Dreadful Sea

Tumbling through the air like a Chinese acrobat, a Naitabal acorn soared across Miss Coates's tall boundary hedge. It struck the top of Ben Tuffin's shed with a hollow "thwack" and bounced off into the unexplored jungle of the garden beyond. Ben was sitting on the seat in his garden. He looked up from his *Beano* in the direction of the Naitabal hut. Another acorn followed, then another, lofted high in the air to fall like hailstones from above. One missed the shed altogether, and one hit the skylight window with a sound like glass cracking. Ben frowned. Cracked glass usually meant awkward questions from parents, probing into things that didn't concern them.

The acorns, lobbed carefully from headquarters, were the signal to Ben that all the Naitabals were back from lunch. It meant the Dreadful Sea was empty of sea-going vessels, and that they were watching through the secret spy-holes.

Ben put down his comic, ready to start. Suddenly, several acorns whizzed in from a different direction. They weren't lobbed gently, but fired with great force from catapults. One stung him on the cheek, making him jump up, one flew past his ear, and one hit him on the shoulder. Another skidded with a loud plop off the *Beano*.

Igmopong!

"Don't be stupid, Cedric Morgan!" Ben said loudly. His voice carried in the still air of the gardens, above the sound of his father sawing wood. "You could blind someone doing that!"

"Not *someone*!" shouted back a thin voice. It floated down from its hiding place somewhere in a tree on Pigmo Island. "*You!*"

Ben turned. The Igmopong, the deadly enemies of the Naitabals, were in the Pigmo tree-house. At least, it was meant to be a tree-house. It was so dilapidated, it looked like a heap of wood that had been sucked up by a whirl-wind and dropped into their tree.

Ben glanced through the rickety splits in their tree-house walls. The four of them were reloading their cata-pults, so he decided to get a move on.

Accomplishing his mission was, of course, a simple matter. All he had to do was to climb Miss Coates's high wall, get through Miss Coates's thick hedge, cross Miss Coates's perfect lawn, and look into Miss Coates's mys-terious well to discover its secret. Then he had to cross Miss Coates's rose bed, squeeze through Miss Coates's other hedge and climb Miss Coates's other wall to get to the Sea of Debris. It was simple, Ben told himself – the only problem was Miss Coates.

In spite of the Naitabals' all-clear, he decided to do his own reconnaissance.

Miss Coates's garden was not an easy one to reconnoitre. It was surrounded on three sides by a high brick wall that Miss Coates's father had built many years before Ben was born, and on the fourth by a high brick wall that Ben's father had built. Added to these, tall hedges had been nurtured and thickened to hide prying eyes from the priv-acy of her garden.

Ben, unperturbed, put some chewing gum into his mouth and climbed on to the high brick wall. With a long broom-handle he parted the bushy branches of the hedge and peered across Miss Coates's garden. It wasn't Miss Coates's garden, of course, and it wasn't a brick wall. Her garden was the Dreadful Sea, and the top of the wall was the highest cliff on Ben Tuffin Island. On Pigmo Island, to his left, the Igmopong had reloaded their catapults and were waiting for the right moment to unleash another volley of acorns.

As Ben's broom-handle parted the tall hedging, Miss Coates was already standing in the middle of her lawn. She was looking disapprovingly up at him along the shaft of the broomstick, her white hair flung out at angles like a wind-swept bush. She had heard the noisy shouts from those awful tree-houses and had come out to investigate. Then she had heard the tell-tale sounds of Ben climbing on to the wall.

Ben, looking down the broom-handle, became uncomfortably aware that an enemy battleship, the SS *Coates*, was close by in the Dreadful Sea. Its deck wore the narrow-eyed and stitched-mouth expression that Ben had tried many times to imitate in front of a mirror, without success. He couldn't make himself look horrible enough.

In the meantime, the ship was becalmed in the Bay of Flowers, and it was starting to make distress signals.

"How dare you sit on my wall," signalled the SS *Coates*. "And how dare you push at my tree with that stick. And how dare you chew that dirty gum stuff."

Ben considered these challenges for a moment. He decided to ignore the first two accusations and answer the third.

"It isn't dirty gum stuff," he protested. To prove this, he used his free hand to pull the gum out at arm's length in a long, drooping string.

"See," he said. "It's clean. It's not dirty at all."

He attempted to fold it back into his mouth. He spent

the next half minute trying to unpeel sticky strands that clung doggedly to his chin.

Miss Coates shuddered, but it was the mere formality of a shudder. Nothing Ben did these days could shock her any more.

To Ben, Miss Coates was simply a sea-going enemy ship, guarding the Dreadful Sea that had to be crossed.

The ship was sending out signals again.

"Get off my wall," it said. "And go away."

Ben frowned.

"In actual fact," he said, in what he hoped was a polite voice, "it's not *your* wall. My Dad says it belongs to us – 'cos he had this one built. Your father built the others." Then he added as a kind afterthought, "But I don't mind if *you* want to sit on it. If you suddenly think you'd like to sit on a wall again, like you did when *you* was a little girl – all those years ago – you just go right ahead. You –"

"*Get off the wall!*"

Ben got off the wall.

A few moments later his persistent voice penetrated the brickwork.

"Of course," he said, "I see what you mean now. It *is* our wall, but when I'm sitting on it, part of me's sort of in your garden, isn't it?" – cheerfully – "Sort of hanging over a bit. You can't sit on a wall without a bit of you hanging over on the other side. And if *you* sat on it, it would be even more." Then he added hastily, "With you being *older*, I mean. I mean, if *none* of me was hanging over your side, I'd be all on my side, and I'd fall off, wouldn't I?"

There was a deep and infuriated silence from the other side of the wall.

"Are you still there?" called Ben in a friendly, chatty voice.

There was no answer.

Ben fetched a small garden bench and propped it

lengthwise against the wall. He hoisted himself up so that his eyes were level with the top of the wall, then gently parted the hedge with his stick. Immediately, he met the grim gun-deck of the SS *Coates*.

"Get down from there!" she snapped.

Ben lowered himself down.

"I wasn't actually *in* your garden that time," he said, by way of explanation. His penetrating voice again floated over the brickwork. "My fingers were on *top* of the wall, and my face was on *my* side. That's all right, isn't it? I wasn't *in* your garden. Or even *over* it. Anyway, when you didn't answer, I thought you might have fainted suddenly . . . "

Again, there was a silence from the other side of the wall. Miss Coates had learned over the years that most forms of conversation with Ben usually made matters far worse in the long run.

"Excuse me, Miss Coates, but are you all right . . . ?" said Ben's voice again, anxiously.

When no answer came, he reached to the top of the wall once more, preparing to hoist himself up for another look. He thought better of it. The prospect of another dose of his neighbour's ugly face was more than he could stand. Anyway, he didn't really care if she *had* fainted. He secretly hoped that she had fallen down her well and would soon be weightless for ever. Serve her right.

With this pleasant thought running through his mind, Ben applied himself again to the problem in hand. The Naitabals were watching all the time – so were the Igmopong – and his reputation was at stake.

He wandered into the house and emerged a few minutes later with a step-ladder. He struggled across the lawn with it, then set it up close to the brick wall further up the garden, making sure that its feet were nice and firm. Holding his broom-handle, he climbed the steps and stood on the little platform at the top. He was slightly higher up now than when he had been sitting on the wall. He gently parted the components of Miss Coates's hedge and surveyed the surrounding terrain. The SS *Coates* had sailed along the Path Canal and was looking straight up the barrel of his 30 mm broomstick gun.

"Get off that ladder, or whatever it is!" said the enemy. "How dare you sit there, staring into my garden. Get down at once!"

"Excuse *me* . . . " began Ben, "but I wasn't looking *in* your garden, I was looking *over* your garden. There's no law against—"

"If you weren't looking into *my* garden," interrupted Miss Coates, "then you must have been looking into someone else's. And if people can't enjoy a bit of privacy in their own garden when it has a six-foot-high wall round it, and nine-foot-high hedges, then I don't know what the country is coming to. Now get down and leave us all in peace and privacy, or I shall speak to your father."

There was a short pause, then Ben said, "*Satellites* can see into your garden. As long as there aren't any clouds in the way, that is. My uncle—"

"*Get down!*"

At this point the alien force seized the far end of his 30 mm broomstick gun. Ben, relinquishing its ownership, nearly fell down the steps with the vigour of this unprovoked attack.

"Charming!" he said in a loud voice. "If you can't even climb up your *own* ladder in your *own* garden, I just *don't know* what the *country* is *coming* to!"

There was a satisfying silence from the Dreadful Sea.

Undaunted by this latest blow to his mission, Ben went into the house again. His father had bought a periscope in an antique shop in Padstow the year before and had given

27

it to Ben in his Christmas stocking. Ben rooted it out and wandered back outside.

He climbed on to the wall and, hidden by the tall hedges, walked all the way to the tree at the end of the garden. He transferred from the wall to the tree, then climbed up as far as he could. With periscope raised, he looked through the eyepiece and saw, very small and rounded, a full view of the enemy's garden. He wondered why he hadn't thought of this before. She couldn't see him, but he could see her. He could see the white blob of its wild hair, the SS *Coates*, heading full steam along the flowerbeds. She was completely unaware that she was being stalked by an enemy submarine. Holding the periscope steady, Ben loosed off one torpedo, then another. He saw the satisfying stream of foam as they surged towards her; saw the spumes of sea and debris as they connected with her hull, and watched her explode in a ball of black smoke and fire before she slowly started sinking . . .

With a sigh, Ben rotated the instrument until he could see the Naitabal tree by the Sea of Debris. He couldn't quite see whether they were still watching him or not, but he knew they would be. They wouldn't miss this adventure for anything. But Ben himself was no nearer the well, and Miss Coates could be in her garden for hours . . .

Suddenly he had a brilliant idea. He climbed down and ran towards his house once more. His father was still sawing wood in the yard, but no one else was around.

He picked up the telephone and dialled Miss Coates's number. Leaving the phone off the hook, he rushed back to the wall. He was just in time to see the SS *Coates* disappearing over the horizon through her french doors.

In a few seconds he was into her garden. It was all neat and tidy, just as he had suspected, perfect in its jealously guarded and boring secrecy. He remembered it vaguely from when he was very small. It was still all lawns and flowerbeds. He ran across them in a straight line towards the Naitabal oak. Miss Coates's telephone had already stopped ringing. She was probably saying "Hello" and beginning to wonder who was trying to call her.

As he passed the middle of her lawn, Ben headed for the well. Suddenly, there was a hail of acorns and voices.

"Oh, Miss Coates, there's a *boy* in your garden!" sang the voices, shrilly, for everyone to hear.

"Oh, Miss Coates, it *looks like* Ben Tuffin!"

Ben ignored the taunts and hurried on. As a toddler, he remembered being forbidden to touch the well or even look into it. He had wondered ever since what it was like inside. He panted up to it, going behind it just in case the SS *Coates* should suddenly reappear.

It was very decorative. It had a circular stone wall for a base, and a tiled roof. Ropes hung down to a bucket suspended at his own eye level. Below the bucket, at the level of the lawn, there was water. In the water were a few goldfish, which shot round in alarm when his head came over the side. He never knew Miss Coates had goldfish!

It wasn't a proper well at all. It was a fake, a dummy. Something to keep goldfish in that looked classy. Ben found himself staring and staring. He *saw* her go down. He *knew* she had. But here was the well with water and goldfish in it. That *must* mean it had a solid base, otherwise all the water would leak down. He took a last anguished look, checked that Miss Coates hadn't returned, then continued his run. It took only a few more seconds to cross her immaculate (until that moment) rose bed, and run to the far corner. He pushed his way through the tall hedge and hoisted himself on to the wall, then leaped diagonally into the Sea of Debris. He let out the cry of the victorious. He acknowledged the cheers of the witnesses above as he stood looking up at the closed trap-door that led to the secret domain of the Naitabals.

On his face was a frown.

CHAPTER THREE

Buried Treasure

Miss Coates walked brisky into her house and answered the telephone. She said "Hello" in a sweet and gentle voice. It wasn't a bit like the carping whine the Naitabals were used to. When there was no answer, but only a strange rasping noise in the earpiece, Miss Coates said "Hello" a little less sweetly. Finally, she said "Hello" with a short, sharp bark, like a Pekinese dog.

The only sound on the line was the raucous sawing noise. There was something suspiciously familiar about it. Miss Coates put the receiver on the hall table and went to stand in the opening of her french doors. She heard the piping chant of a voice saying "Oh, Miss Coates, it *looks like* Ben Tuffin!" Then she saw a flash of yellow jumper, with boy above and boy below, disappearing into the high hedge in the corner of her garden.

"So!" she said to herself.

From next door came the sound made by Ben's father, Mr Tuffin, sawing wood. It was exactly the same sound that was coming through on the telephone. Miss Coates strode back to the earpiece to check. Sure enough, when Mr Tuffin stopped sawing, the noise on the telephone stopped. When Mr Tuffin started sawing again, the noise on the telephone started again.

Miss Coates's chest swelled with fury. She left her telephone off the hook and marched next door. She pushed the bell and knocked the knocker simultaneously. The sawing noise stopped and Ben's father appeared at the door. He was a mild and easy-going man, but when he saw who was calling he smiled a sickly smile of recognition.

"Ah, Miss Coates, it's you."

"Yes, Mr Tuffin."

There was something about Miss Coates's face that told him this was not a social call. But then, it never was. None of Miss Coates's calls were social calls. They were always about Ben.

"Do come in," sighed Mr Tuffin.

She came in.

"There!" she said suddenly. She pointed accusingly at the telephone that lay off its hook.

"Where?" said Mr Tuffin. He looked round, mystified.

"There!" said Miss Coates, pointing more viciously.

"The telephone?" suggested Mr Tuffin.

"Yes, Mr Tuffin. *Your telephone*."

Ben's father waited patiently, hoping for enlightenment. Conversations with Miss Coates were always spent waiting patiently, hoping for enlightenment. She never seemed to get to the point. But this time his patience was not wasted. Miss Coates began to roll towards him like a Centurion Tank.

"Your son," she said, "has just telephoned my number."

Again, Mr Tuffin said nothing at first. Ben telephoning her number seemed rather odd, but not a great crime. He was about to put this thought politely into words when, luckily for him, he received further information from Miss Coates.

"Your son Benjamin *rang* my number, Mr Tuffin, so that I would *vacate* my garden and go into the house. With me out of the way, he could *climb* the wall, make a *hole* in my hedge, *trudge* across my lovely lawn, and *trample* on my rose bed. And all for a rendezvous with the hooligan inhabitants of that *outrageous* tree-house."

"Oh, dear," began Mr Tuffin apologetically, but his

words were swept away as the storm raged on.

"If I hadn't put my foot down with that fool Eddie Elliott, the tree-house would have had *windows* overlooking my private garden. Why he built it and allows them to play there, I shall *never* understand. What have you got to say about *that*, Mr Tuffin?"

Mr Tuffin, already shouted down once, didn't know where to begin.

"Er – you're sure it was Ben, I suppose?" he suggested weakly, seeing a possible way out. He soon regretted suggesting any such thing.

"Pick up your telephone!" commanded Miss Coates, storming out of the house. "And keep it picked up!"

Mr Tuffin obeyed. He picked it up and kept it picked up. Suddenly Miss Coates's voice came through with a high-pitched shrill, like a gnat trapped in his ear.

"Are we connected, Mr Tuffin?" said the screech. "Or are we not?"

For one mad moment, Mr Tuffin was tempted to say "Oi'm zorry but youze gott a crosst loine" in a funny accent and gently replace the receiver. But he had long been a coward where Miss Coates was concerned. The temptation passed.

"Yes, we're connected, Miss Coates," he said with a sigh. "I'm very sorry, and I'll talk to Ben when he gets back."

"And another thing," said the shrill voice. Then there was a loud crack in the earpiece. Just as Mr Tuffin was beginning to say "Hello" to a dead line, Miss Coates reappeared at his front door carrying a broom-handle. He hoped she would sit on it and fly off with the cat.

"I also caught him standing on the *wall* earlier!" She said it in a rush, as if she had been holding her breath since slamming down the receiver. "He was looking into my garden by pushing *this* through the hedge." She thrust the broom-handle at him. "I will *not* have my privacy abused in this way! Under no circumstances is your son *or anybody else*, to *spy* on my garden. Is that understood?"

"Oh, yes," said Mr Tuffin. He had already started dreaming up suitable punishments for Ben. "Yes, I do understand, Miss Coates. It must be very annoying for you, and I'll talk to him the moment he gets in."

Miss Coates fixed Mr Tuffin with a gimlet eye.

"Then that's settled," she said. "Perhaps I can get back to my garden. And the sooner we have that tree-house removed, the better!"

Still frowning, Ben stood behind the trunk of the great Naitabal oak waiting for the rope ladder to be lowered. The jeering voices of the Igmopong – ducked like cowards behind the fence that separated Pigmo Island from the Sea of Debris – floated across the chicken run.

"We saw you going across Miss Coates's garden!" shouted Cedric Morgan, their leader, deliberately loud in the hope that Miss Coates could still hear them.

"You looked in her well!" shrilled Amanda Wilson.

"You trampled in her rose bed!" piped another voice, Doris Morgan this time, Cedric's bossy sister.

Ben looked up at the protective branches of the Naitabal oak spread like the wings of a giant eagle. Above him, nailed to the trunk, was the sign in Naitabal language:

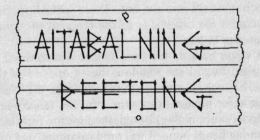

and below that, in blood-red paint:

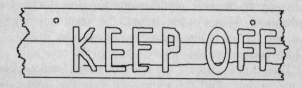

He felt safe behind the trunk, but he'd be even safer once he was beyond the trap-door of the Naitabal hut. The only problem was climbing the rope ladder with the Igmopong around.

Next to the trap-door above his head hung a bell on a piece of string. Ben delved into his pocket. He wriggled out his catapult and a big acorn, loaded it, and aimed at the bell. He fired. The acorn lofted skywards and missed. He tried another. That missed as well, rattling on the underside of the hut. The third made the bell ring with a satisfying little dance. That was the signal. The trap-door wouldn't open unless you rang the bell first, however much danger you were in. It was just one of the rules.

He heard the sound of bolts being withdrawn above, then watched as slowly, very slowly, the trap-door began to open upwards into the hut. There was whispering and scuffling on the other side of the fence as the Igmopong prepared to attack.

He stood back as the rope ladder was lowered down. He heard two of the windows being opened in the hut above him, then a shouted "Go!" from the Naitabals. At the same moment two acorns hit the fence where the Igmopong were hiding. Ben dashed for the rope ladder as Igmopong heads popped up, fired catapults, and dropped down. A hail of acorns filled the air in both directions. Some hit Ben as he climbed – one hit his bare hand, two hit his legs. Someone scored a direct hit on Cedric Morgan. His furious red face appeared over the fence and unleashed another vicious attack. Cries and laughter filled the still air of the gardens. The battle was a formality, but it was always exciting. Sometimes the Naitabals won, keeping the Igmopong pinned behind their fence; sometimes the Igmopong won, preventing a Naitabal from climbing the ladder until their ammunition ran out.

Ben stood for a second swaying on a middle rung, savouring the precious moments of glory as acorns whizzed about him. This time the enemy was forced to retreat.

He climbed up towards the trap-door and disappeared into the Naitabal hut, eager to tell the others what he had seen in the well.

At about the time that Ben was firing acorns at the Naitabal bell, a car was moving slowly along Meadow Lane. The driver, Mr Blake, was looking for Bluebell Cottage, where Miss Coates lived. He was not looking forward to meeting his cousin again. It was fifty years since he had seen her. Given the choice, he would have been quite happy not to see her for another fifty.

As his car rounded the bend that brought Bluebell Cottage into view, he saw her. She hadn't been nice to look at when she was ten, and she wasn't nice to look at now. She was marching down the steps of the house next door, brandishing a broom-handle, and looking furious. She was just the same, and he laughed. It was as if the fifty years had never been. She was still thin and shapeless, and her hair still stuck out as it always had, except that now it was brilliant white, like candy floss.

He parked his car and approached the house, the front

door already slammed. He got a smile ready and rang the bell.

The face that appeared was flustered and cross, but it changed quickly to a look of surprise, then mild pleasure.

"Oh – Charles! You're here already!" She smiled a weak, welcoming smile. "I was expecting you, of course, but I quite lost track of the time!"

"Hello, Edith," said Mr Blake. "It's lovely to see you after all these years."

They shook hands and he kissed her on her fluffy cheek, like kissing a pink marshmallow.

"Been having trouble with the neighbours?" he asked.

"Oh, nothing much, really," she said, inviting him inside. "Their ten-year-old son is a handful, that's all. He needs keeping in check."

Mr Blake smiled. She should be good at that, he thought, but he said, "Oh, well. You know what children are like!"

"I know what *you* were like!" said Miss Coates, without humour.

She led him into the sitting room. Through the open french window came the sounds of the battle: shrill voices, jeers, shouts, cries of pain and anger, the swish of elastic and the slap of missiles hitting wood.

Without a word, Miss Coates closed the french doors, and the sounds all but disappeared. It was an automatic action she did so often without thinking.

"Let's have a cup of tea first . . . Have you had lunch?"

After a cup of tea, Mr Blake sat back in his chair and explained his problem.

"I didn't know I had a problem," he said, "until Mother died. And yet it's come at the right time. *Exactly* the right time."

Miss Coates sighed.

"You said in your letter it was something in your mother's will?"

"Yes. It said that your father buried a box of family papers in the garden during the war. To protect them if a bomb hit the house."

"I see," said Miss Coates. "And what was supposed to be in the box?"

"Money – in the form of bonds and share certificates. As you know, my parents lived in a rented house at the time. They obviously felt safer with their important papers buried in a strong box rather than lying around under a bed. Father died just after the war – we children were told nothing about the box – and it's only mother's will that has brought the thing to light."

Miss Coates laughed an unkind laugh. "And you've travelled two hundred miles to tell me that?"

Mr Blake was slightly disconcerted.

"I need those papers."

"Why?"

"I'm desperate for the money. The only thing I don't understand is why my parents didn't insist on having them back after the war."

"*It's already been done, Charles.*"

"You mean you've found the box?" – a brief glimmer of hope.

"No. The garden was dug up immediately after the war. The box had gone – it wasn't where my father buried it. There was a terrible fuss! The whole garden was *turned over*. It was dug to a depth of several feet in all sorts of places, rods were pushed into the soil – *everything*, Charles. *They couldn't find the box.* Accusations were made. Someone must have stolen it during the war. *It wasn't there*, Charles."

"Can't we have just one more try . . . ?"

Miss Coates turned her eyes to the french windows.

"Just look at the garden now, Charles. I've spent half

my life making it beautiful – it's really all I have, you know. I couldn't *bear* to have it dug up and messed about with now. I couldn't *bear* it."

Mr Blake rose and went to stand at the window.

"It's very secluded, isn't it?" he said conversationally. "Anyone would think you'd got something to hide."

There was a pause – slight but unmistakable.

"It's those beastly children," said Miss Coates hurriedly.

"I know how you feel about the garden, Edith. But the bonds were given to Uncle Harold for safe keeping – and I've a *right* to have them back."

Miss Coates remained motionless, deep in thought. At last she said, "Can't the money be claimed without the paperwork? Aren't there any other records?"

"We've no way of knowing without the box."

"How bad is this financial trouble, Charles?"

Her cousin sighed.

"I'll lose my house if I don't get it. That hidden box is my lifeboat."

"*You're not digging up my garden, Charles.*"

"But I *must*. I have to find it."

"Well, you can't."

Mr Blake looked at her long and hard. It was as if they were children again. She was stubborn and argumentative then, and she hadn't changed a bit. Distract her. Cheer her up.

"Oh, look! A tree-house!" he said, pointing. It was overdone, but so what? She'd remember. "Better than the rickety thing we had – don't you think?" He turned to look at Miss Coates. There was no smile. Evidently, she didn't think.

"Eddie Elliott built it," she said sharply.

"What – little Eddie?"

"Little Eddie," she reminded him, "is sixty."

"Oh, yes. I suppose he would be. I must pop round and

38

see him while I'm here. We had great fun in the tree-house when we were young, didn't we?"

Miss Coates's expression changed from displeasure to fury. She denied that she had *ever* been young herself, or had any fun. She told him at brain-deadening length what she thought of Eddie Elliott – and the tree-house – and the children who inhabited it.

The tirade ended, and Mr Blake suddenly brightened.

"I know!" he said. "We needn't disturb the garden at all! I'll get one of those people to go round with a divining rod. They'll find *anything* under the ground!"

To his surprise, he just caught a flicker of fear on his cousin's face. Then it was gone.

"Those things are nonsense!" she said. But she didn't convince herself, or her visitor.

Mr Blake looked again at the tall hedges and trees that surrounded her garden. From that moment he *knew* she was hiding something.

CHAPTER FOUR

Naitabal Language

Helping hands pulled Ben into the Naitabal hut amid a hail of acorns, and closed the trap-door. A few final missiles rattled on the underside of the floor, then subsided.

Everyone said "Well done!" and there were smiles all round.

"*Igmo-pong atch-wung!*" warned Boff, before anyone said anything else.

Jayne didn't understand Naitabal language, but the others told her it meant "Pigmo watch". Toby, nearest the south window, turned to look out at Pigmo Island.

"All clear," he announced. "All four of them have gone into their tree."

"Good."

While Toby stayed on Pigmo watch, they all turned to Ben. They were going to teach Jayne Naitabal language, but Ben knew they'd all want to know about the well first.

"The well's got goldfish in it," he said, without wasting any time.

"What do you mean," said Toby, "it's got goldfish in it?"

Ben raised his eyebrows.

"I mean – *it's got goldfish in it.*"

"You mean right down at the bottom, where the water is?"

"No."

"Where, then?"

"Right at the *top*, where the water is."

"At the *top*?"

"It's a dummy. Like I said this morning. It isn't really a well at all."

"You mean, she couldn't have gone down it?" said Toby, still keeping a careful eye out of the window.

"But she *did* go down it. You know she did. I saw her go down, and you and me saw her come up."

"And you're *sure* there were fish in it?" said Boff, stirring out of a thoughtful silence.

Ben was starting to get irritated. Then Charlotte said, "There's something fishy about that well!" and a great groan went up from the assembled company.

"Of course I'm sure," said Ben, calming down. "Why doesn't anyone believe me? Anyone'd think I was always telling lies."

There was a brief silence, then Charlotte said, "We do believe you, Ben, of course we do. It's just that it's all so odd. There must be some explanation."

"We think she saw you," said Jayne suddenly, speaking for the first time.

Ben turned his head sharply.

"Miss Coates?"

"Yes. Just after you'd finished looking in the well, she came to her french door and saw you."

Ben shrugged.

"Oh, well. She'll probably tell my father. She'd have found out anyway with the Igmopong shouting it all over the place. It'd be just like them to call and tell her straight off."

"Anyway – well done, Ben," said Boff. "It looks as though the well needs further investigation. Perhaps we'll be able to use *Roject-pong Ubmarine-song*."

"Where there's a well there's a way," said Charlotte, grinning through the cave in her teeth. It produced another groan from the Naitabals.

41

"What on earth is *Roject-pong Ub-whatever-you-said*?" said Jayne, totally mystified.

"It's Naitabal Language," said Boff. "The same as *Igmo-pong* and *Aitabal-ning ree-tong*."

"Oh, yes. That's what's written on the tree. And you all understand it?"

"*Es-yung!*" said the others in unison.

"Sounds like it's time I learnt some, then," said Jayne.

"Yes," said Charlotte. "But we've got to swear you in as a Naitabal first."

"Of course. I'd forgotten that," said Jayne. Her bright blue eyes darted round the hut. "Are there any more things to show me, like the peep-holes for spying on Miss Coates's garden?"

"Maybe," said Charlotte. She took up a piece of paper from the wide window ledge where Boff had begun quietly writing and drawing. "Repeat after me. Naitabals can do anything."

"Naitabals can do anything," repeated Jayne.

"Naitabals can go anywhere," said Charlotte.

"Naitabals can go anywhere."

"Naitabals never break the law . . . "

"Naitabals never break the law . . . "

" . . . Unless it's absolutely necessary . . . "

" . . . Unless it's absolutely necessary . . . "

"Naitabals sometimes go to bed with their clothes on."

"What on earth for?" said Jayne.

"Never mind what for," said Toby. "You'll find out later. Just repeat the oath."

"Naitabals sometimes go to bed with their clothes on."

"Naitabals are always kind and considerate to brothers, sisters, and parents."

"Naitabals are always kind and considerate to brothers, sisters, and parents."

"Except when under extreme pressure."

"Except when under extreme pressure."

"What does that mean?" said Jayne, interrupting before the next oath.

"Never mind what it means. You've sworn it now, so you can't go back on it as long as you're a Naitabal."

"All right."

"Naitabals wear natural materials and only eat people," chanted Charlotte.

"Naitabals wear natural materials and only eat – did you say *people*?" – the last word in a shocked voice.

"Except when under extreme pressure."

"Does 'Except when under extreme pressure' come into it a lot?" asked Jayne.

"Yes. So you'd better just say it. You're not supposed to ask silly questions."

"Sorry. Except when under extreme pressure."

"Naitabals never ask silly questions," put in Toby.

"I bet you've just made that one up," Jayne protested. There was a silence as she looked at the serious faces around her. "Naitabals never ask silly questions, then," she said.

"Except when under extreme pressure."

Jayne was about to repeat this doggedly, when all the others suddenly started laughing. Before she could quite understand, and join in the laughter herself, Toby said quickly, "Naitabals can always take a joke."

Jayne grinned.

"Naitabals can always take a joke," she said. "Is that it?"

"No. There are two more. The most important one of all: all Naitabal activities are secret."

"All Naitabal activities are secret."

"And Naitabals are kind to the Earth."

"And Naitabals are kind to the Earth."

"That's why we eat people," said Toby. "Especially people like the Igmopong."

"Good," said Charlotte. "Now you're sworn in."

43

Jayne grinned.

"Thanks."

"If you're needed for an emergency meeting, the big Naitabal bell will be rung." Charlotte pointed to the bell which hung from the middle of the roof.

"OK."

"I've told you about emergencies. If you're needed for an ordinary meeting, a Naitabal acorn will land in the raintub next to your garden shed. You'll have to keep it topped up with water. And you'll have to know everyone else's target. Mine is the Naitabal lagoon on Charlotte Island. It's quite a long way off, but at least it's a big target. Toby has a bell hanging on his mother's washing line – which doesn't matter because Toby's mother never washes any clothes, anyway."

Toby laughed his funny silent laugh.

"Ben's is the roof of his garden shed, because no other part of his garden is visible from here," Charlotte went on. She pointed out the target through one of the windows.

Jayne turned and gave Ben a brief little smile.

"And Boff's is his bedroom window. You *have to* use a catapult to call Boff, but he assures us it won't break the glass."

"What if someone's not at home?"

"We leave three Naitabal acorns on your front door-step," said Toby.

"We'll teach you Naitabal language next," said Charlotte. "I'll teach you, because I'm best."

Jayne opened her eyes wide as if in protest. She had not realised before joining the Naitabals that there was such a thing as Naitabal language.

"Me learn the whole language? But I'm hopeless at languages."

"Don't worry," said Toby. "This one's easy to learn."

"A child of ten can do it," said Ben, grinning.

44

"No adults can understand what we're saying, that's the main thing."

"We can say things to each other in front of our parents, and they haven't got a clue what we're talking about," said Charlotte, grinning.

Boff slowly and deliberately looked up from his diagrams, and announced stiffly, "We only use it in emergencies. It would take loads of practice to speak it all the time."

"How long does it take to learn the whole language?" said Jayne, worried. She had visions of spending night after night learning nouns and verbs by the hundred.

"About five minutes," said Charlotte. "You don't have to *learn* it. You only have to learn *how* to speak it."

"I don't understand."

"I'll explain. If you want to say 'dog' in Naitabal, you take off the first letter and say 'og'."

"Og," said Jayne. "That's easy."

"Then you take the first letter and stick it on the end and say 'og-d'."

"Og-d."

"And then you just add 'ang' on the end and say *og-dang*."

"*Og-dang*."

"So 'cat' in Naitabal is *at-cang*."

"*At-cang*. I see." Now it was Jayne's turn to grin. "It's easy."

"Yes," said Charlotte, pulling a mock serious face. "The only trouble is, we have five different endings."

"Five?"

" 'Ang' you've learnt. Then there are 'eng', 'ing', 'ong', and 'ung'."

"Oh, dear!"

"If the word starts with a, b, c or d, like cat or dog, you end the Naitabal word with 'ang' – *at-cang* and *og-dang*. If

45

it starts with e, f, g or h, you add 'eng'. So fish is *ish-feng*, and garden is *arden-geng*."

Jayne was looking slightly confused again, so Charlotte took a piece of paper and drew a chart:

Starting letter	Ending
a,b,c,d	ang
e,f,g,h	eng
i,j,k,l,m,n	ing
o,p,q,r,s,t	ong
u,v,w,x,y,z	ung

"So 'moon' is *oon-ming*," said Jayne, getting the idea.

"That's right!"

"And 'sun' is *un-song*."

"Yep!"

"And 'wild' is *ild-wung*!"

"Hooray!" shouted the Naitabals. "She's got it!"

"I said a child of ten could do it!" said Ben.

Then Charlotte said, "We've got the Naitabal Chant to help us remember. Let's do it, so Jayne can learn the endings."

"OK," said Toby. "It's all clear on the Pigmo front."

The Naitabals gathered round the centre of the hut, with their hands flat on the floor, and Jayne copied them. Boff stayed at his desk, too deep in thought to join in.

Then Charlotte began the chant.

"A, B, C, D!"

The Naitabals slapped the floor and shouted in unison: "ANG!"

"E, F, G, H!"

Again the floor was slapped and the cry rang out: "ENG!"

"I, J, K, L, M, N!"

"ING!"

"O, P, Q, R, S, T!"

"ONG!"

"U, V, W, X, Y, Z!"

"UNG!"

It was a primeval chant: a Naitabal song steeped in ancient Naitabal lore. With the final explosive syllable they all slapped the floor for the last time, and patchy giggling broke out.

Jayne stood up and pointed at the trap-door.

"*Rap-tong Oor-dang!*" she said, slowly.

There was a burst of spontaneous applause.

She pointed to the window.

"*Indow-Wung,*" she said.

Another round of applause.

"I said you'd get it in five minutes," said Charlotte, proud of her new pupil.

Jayne indicated the floor.

"*Oor-fleng!*" she said.

"No," said Toby. "You only take off the first letter. Floor is *Loor-feng.*"

Jayne nodded.

"There's only three other rules," said Charlotte. "If a word starts with a, e, i, o or u, you don't take it off the front – so 'ant' is *ant-ang.*"

"Right."

"If a word starts with 'ch', 'sh', 'th' or 'wh', you take both letters off the front – so 'ship' is *ip-shong.*"

"Got it."

"And last of all, the word 'I' is *Ing*, and 'a' is *ang.*"

"Wow!"

They all got up, except Boff, and squashed themselves against a window to look for inspiration.

Toby pointed to the next door cat and said, "*Ussy-pong!*" and they all started to giggle.

"*Obin-rong,*" said Charlotte, spotting a bird.

"*Lackbird-bang!*" said Ben, spotting another.

"*Icken-chang,*" said Jayne.

Then Boff stirred and said, "I wish you lot would *ut-shong up-ung* so *Ing* can *ink-thong*!"

"What are you actually doing?" said Toby.

"Just a slight adjustment to *Roject-pong Ubmarine-song*," said Boff, stretching, but would say no more.

"Project Submarine!" said Jayne, then added, "What-ever *that* is!"

No one decided to enlighten her, and before she could wonder much what it was, Toby, who was back on Pigmo watch, suddenly whispered fervently, "*Igmo-pong*!"

Jayne suddenly realised that Igmopong was a Naitabal word. She quickly translated it back to "Pigmo". Pigmo Island!

"What's a Pigmo?" she said.

"Lawns, mostly," said Charlotte, starting to giggle. That set Toby off as well.

While they were laughing, Boff said, "Where are they?"

"The Igmopong? Coming back towards the fence," Toby said. "All four of them. Hoping to listen in, probably."

Jayne, having no luck with getting serious answers from the others, looked out of the window herself. They were easy enough to see. They were creeping across Pigmo Island, using what they probably imagined was secrecy and stealth. The whole gang was there – Cedric and Doris Morgan and Andy and Amanda Wilson.

"*Why* do you call them 'Pigmo'?" she said.

That started Charlotte giggling again, but Toby spoke up in a quiet, ironic voice.

"Because Cedric's small, like a Pigmy, and Pigmo in Naitabal is *Igmo-pong*, and that's a cross between a pigmy, an ignoramus, a pig and a pong! It describes the four of them perfectly!"

Jayne knew exactly what he meant. Cedric Morgan was small, and tried to make up for it by being aggressive. His red-headed sister Doris was also aggressive, but had no brains at all. Amanda was tubby, ate like a pig, and spent most of her spare time pushing her brother Andy around. Andy was dim, skinny, and smelt like a cheese factory.

"Just keep quiet for a bit," said Boff, "and perhaps they'll go away."

"Judging by the stupid grin on Cedric Morgan's face," said Toby, "I'd say they were planning something."

CHAPTER FIVE

Igmopong
and Idnap-king

"I want to talk to you."

The words, delivered by Ben's father, descended upon Ben like a raincloud as he entered the kitchen for tea. At first glance, there had been nothing wrong. His mother was dancing round the kitchen pretending to be Julie Andrews, singing "The grills are alive, with a round of toast in," and Mr Tuffin was just replacing the telephone. On second glance, however, it looked as if his father hadn't had any sleep for three nights.

Ben's mind raced back over the events of the morning, searching for something he'd done that might have upset anybody. The report about Miss Coates seeing him in her garden had long faded from his mind. He had spent the whole day initiating Jayne as a Naitabal. They couldn't possibly know anything about that. Anyway, the Naitabals hadn't done anything *wrong*.

"I have had *four* separate complaints from Miss Coates," his father proceeded. "I'm fairly used by now to having *one* complaint a week, but when I get four in one morning, it's a bit much."

"*Four*?" was all Ben could think of to say. He was genuinely surprised that there could have been even one. Well, maybe he could think of perhaps *one*, but *four* . . . Gradually, a memory came back to him, "I only sat on the wall and looked across her garden," he protested.

"Oh, that's five, then," said Mr Tuffin impassively. "I've told you lots of times before not to climb on the wall and annoy our neighbours." He paused to see if Ben would come up with any more confessions.

"Then when she told me to get down, I looked at her through my periscope . . . "

"Six."

Slowly, it began to occur to Ben that this voluntary confession of crimes was not a good idea. He decided to let justice do its own dirty work.

"What did she complain about, then?" he said.

"First of all, that your friends were throwing acorns at her."

"Well, that wasn't me! I can't help it if the dopey Igmo – I mean Cedric Morgan and his gang – throw acorns at her, can I? Anyway, they weren't throwing them at her."

"Who were they throwing them at, then?"

"Me."

"Oh, I see. Nice friends."

"Cedric Morgan isn't a *friend*!" said Ben vehemently. He decided not to explain further. "What else did she say I did?"

"How about marching across her rose bed? Does that sound familiar?"

Ben had a vague recollection of being among roses at some time during the day.

"It's possible . . . " he began, but Mr Tuffin held up a hand.

"No," he said. "Don't explain. I don't think I could bear one of your explanations. It was the malice aforethought that really upset her."

"The Alice who?" said Ben, screwing up his face.

"You heard. The malice aforethought. Using the telephone to distract her attention and get her inside the

51

house. So that you could do your dirty work of rose-trampling."

Ben was flabbergasted. How on earth could they know about the telephone? He'd only rung her number. She couldn't possibly have known who *wasn't* on the other end of a telephone line . . . But then another vision suddenly came into his mind's eye. It was a little picture of a telephone receiver left off the hook in a familiar hall . . .

"Your mistake," said Mr Tuffin slowly, "was in not understanding how the telephone system works."

"Oh?"

"They haven't yet invented a system where telephone receivers put themselves back on."

"Aah!" said Ben.

"Yes," said Mr Tuffin, grim-faced. "Aah!"

There was a short silence.

"The fourth complaint came when Miss Coates rang a few moments ago to say that you have just tried, for the second time, to create a right-of-way across her rose bed. She fears that if you continue to do this for another thirty years, it will become a public footpath."

Ben was going to say "Really?" but suddenly realised that the last bit was his father being sarcastic.

"Sorry, Dad," he said instead. His second visit to the well had been no more rewarding than the first. It was still full of goldfish.

"On this occasion, I'm afraid, 'Sorry' will not be enough. You are not to go across Miss Coates's garden again, or to climb over *any* of the other garden walls or fences, or to walk along them. You are banned from watching television for a week."

"But, Dad . . . !"

"I don't care what you'll miss," said Mr Tuffin. "And no video recording, either. If you want to avoid the confiscation of these little pleasures in future, you must learn to respect your neighbours' property. Understood?"

"Yes, Dad."

In the background, his mother was still being Julie Andrews, but this time she was singing "A spoonful of vinegar helps the sausages go bro-own."

After tea, Ben set off for the Naitabal oak the long way round.

At first he was a speedboat, speeding along the edge of the Meadow Lane-ian Sea, past Coates's harbour, and on towards Toby Island. Then he decided to slow down and be a frogman, but just as he did he saw Toby. Toby was climbing out of his front window straight into a flowerbed. He had nothing on his feet, and his hair wasn't brushed.

Ben stopped. "Why are you coming out of the window?" he said. He might not have bothered asking, because Toby was always doing strange things.

"Oh, the front door's jammed," said Toby, shrugging. "It's been like that for ages."

"You mean you have to get in and out like that all the time?"

"Yes."

"You can't use the front door at all?"

"No. And the back door only goes into the garden."

"What does your mother do, then? Does she have to go in and out?"

"Yep. She goes in and out of the window as well. If we wait here a minute, we'll see her. She's going shopping soon."

Within seconds, Mrs Hamilton's plump form appeared at the open window. Luckily, it was a Victorian house and the windows were large. The boys were treated to the sight of Toby's mother's ungainly shape puffing its way over the window sill. She dropped into the flowerbed, then straightened her rather tight overcoat. She went off down the road with a swank as if she had just stepped out of a Rolls Royce.

"Well!" said Ben. "How long's it been like that?"

"Oh, about three months," said Toby.

"Why doesn't your father fix it?"

"Father?" said Toby, rhetorically.

Ben thought of Mr Hamilton, well known in the district as an ace layabout, and realised what a stupid question it was.

"Doesn't your mother *mind*?" he said instead.

"Keeps her fit," said Toby, simply.

They started to walk along the edge of the Meadow Lane-ian Sea, turning left at Corner Island where it flowed into the Avenue Canal, and on past Spider Island where two of the Igmopong, Andy and Amanda Wilson, lived.

Ben decided to ask about Toby's footwear.

"You haven't got anything on your feet," he said, as if noticing it for the first time. "Where are your shoes?"

"Couldn't find 'em," said Toby, simply.

Ben conjured up a memory of the contents of Toby's house, and wasn't surprised.

They turned left into the Straits of Brunswick and sailed on past Boff Island, which was next to Mr Elliott's garden where the Naitabal oak tree stood.

The entrance to Mr Elliott's garden was always easy to recognise. Most front gardens in the Straits of Brunswick had walls, gates or hedges, but Mr Elliott's had cracked concrete, weeds, and a big yellow skip. The skip was full of rubbish, and the garden was full of rubbish. If it wasn't for the glimpses of yellow paint, it was impossible to tell where the skip ended and the front garden began. The first living thing in sight was the old lilac tree. It had a wooden sign nailed to its trunk at a drunken angle, announcing:

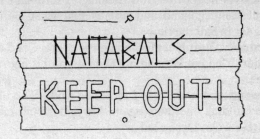

The word NAITABALS was written carefully in black to look like spears and arrows. KEEP OUT was scrawled boldly with red paint that had run like blood down the sign. It was a warning to anyone thinking of trespassing.

Mr Elliott himself was a man of roughly sixty. He was a builder, he was bald, and he was always covered in dust. Ben couldn't remember a time when he had ever seen him not covered in dust. Mr Elliott worked at building seven days a week. When it was light and not raining, he worked outside. When it was dark or raining, he worked inside. He lived alone, and he only visited his house to do three things: to eat, to sleep, and to deposit rubbish. He didn't eat much, he didn't sleep much, but he deposited a lot of rubbish. The rest of the time he was working.

Boff's garden was next door to his, and Boff had long used Mr Elliott's garden as a place to be alone. He also used it to obtain material for any project he was engaged upon. When he needed a galvanised bath to make a submarine for the lagoon on Charlotte Island, he had found one among Mr Elliott's rubbish. (The submarine was very successful and stayed under water even longer than planned.) And when Boff needed to make the rope bridge from the tree in his own garden across to the Naitabal oak, he had found plenty of rope.

The nice thing about Mr Elliott was that he never

objected to Boff's activities, but actually encouraged them. If ever he spotted Boff rummaging through a heap, he would lend a hand and usually find what Boff was looking for in half the time.

Eventually, Boff had plucked up the courage and asked Mr Elliott if he could build a tree-house in his enormous oak tree.

"A wonderful idea!" Mr Elliott had said. "I've always fancied building one there again. Me father built me one in that tree when I was a lad."

Mr Elliott had started work on it there and then. He stopped working for a whole week (without giving his customers any notice or warning) and built the tree-house with his own hands. He used the best and strongest wood from his seemingly limitless pile, and he made the perfect tree-house. Then, when it was finished, he had returned (without notice or warning) to his mystified customers.

Ben and Toby, standing now on top of a heap of bricks near the skip, gazed for a moment down the garden at the incredible amount of wood and rubbish. But it wasn't wood and rubbish, of course: it was the Sea of Debris.

Then Jayne joined them as well, and the three of them began to pick their way over the heap. They soon reached the winding path, much easier on Toby's feet. After stopping to get a splinter out of his foot, Toby said, "Boff isn't there, yet. Look. The rope ladder's not down."

Jayne frowned. "Well, how does Boff get in, then? And how does he stop anyone else getting in when he's not there?"

"Easy." Toby pointed.

Jayne's eye followed his arm to the rope contraption that stretched from the Naitabal oak and disappeared into the tree in the corner of Boff Island.

"When Boff leaves," said Ben, "he pulls up the rope ladder. Then he locks the trap-door and goes out through the hatch in the roof."

"Good grief!"

"He padlocks it so no one can get in, then he crosses the Naitabal bridge to his own tree, and climbs down."

"So that's how we stop the Igmopong getting in and doing mischief!"

"They'll never get into the hut," said Toby. "The only way is through Boff's garden – and they haven't got a key. And they'd never get past us, Boff's parents, *and* his alsatian!"

"Let's go and see if Charlotte's ready," said Ben.

"You go," said Toby. "I'll stay here and look for some old shoes in the skip."

"Do you get all your shoes from the skip?" said Jayne, shocked.

"You can find all sorts of things," said Toby.

"I'll stay and help you search, then," said Jayne.

Ben went cautiously along the road past the Pigmo's house. He was ready for an ambush by the Igmopong at any second, but nothing happened. He went in through Charlotte's side gate and spotted her down by Charlotte Lagoon with her seven-year-old brother, Harry.

Ben liked Charlotte. She was a special friend and as good as a boy any day. Her only disadvantage was her small brother, who was spoilt, tubby and generally a nuisance. Charlotte's parents believed in their children being independent, which meant that they didn't want to see Charlotte or Harry except at meal times. Harry was far too young to be a Naitabal, so he usually had to be "disposed of" by Charlotte. But sometimes she was stuck with him, and though he made a nuisance of himself, she usually managed to put up with him.

Ben took a Naitabal acorn from his pocket and lofted it high into the air. It fell with a light smack on the grass near the pond and made Harry look up into the sky.

"Something fell down," he announced.

Charlotte, who knew what it must have been, did nothing.

Ben tried a few times more until one acorn dropped with a satisfying ploop into the pond. Charlotte immediately got up and ran towards him, laughing.

"Only five tries. That was good!" she said.

Ben smiled. "Boff's not there yet," he said. "Do you want to come round now and wait?"

"I'll have to do something with Harry."

Charlotte glanced over her shoulder. Harry was standing in the pond. There was black slime up the backs of both his legs and on his hands and wrists. One hand held a jam jar on a piece of string, full of murky water, and the other was stirring the pond with a big stick.

"Poor goldfish," murmured Ben.

"Oh, Harry's all right," said Charlotte, deciding. "He won't make a fuss if he doesn't actually see me go."

They crept off Charlotte Island together. By the time they reached the Naitabal oak, Boff, Toby and Jayne were already there, and the rope ladder was waiting for them. There was no sign of the Igmopong.

Charlotte's first duty on climbing inside was to look out of the south window to see if Harry had missed her. She screamed with delight.

"I don't believe it!"

The other Naitabals rushed to the window to see what was happening.

Cedric Morgan, the chief of the Igmopong, did not possess the speediest brain on Earth. When he first had the idea of kidnapping Charlotte's seven-year-old brother Harry, he had visions of the victim bound and gagged in their tree-house. He also imagined Charlotte standing in the garden below, begging them to release her poor little brother in return for anything they wanted.

What happened in reality was very different.

As soon as they had seen Harry deserted by his big sister, Cedric and Andy had climbed the fence into Charlotte's garden. Stealthily, they approached their victim. There were two of *them*, and one of Harry. *Their* ages added up to twenty-one. Harry's didn't need adding up: it was seven on its own. There was nothing to it.

"You've gotta come with us," said Cedric in an authoritarian sort of voice.

"Don't want to," said Harry, without looking up. "Wanter stay here wiv fishes."

"You've gotta leave the fish here and come with us."

"Don't want to. Fishin'."

"You've gotta come," said Cedric, more threateningly. "Otherwise . . . " he felt that leaving the sentence unfinished was more menacing.

Harry called his bluff.

"Uvverwise wot?" he said.

Cedric, who hadn't actually planned what would happen to Harry if he refused, stalled for time.

"Never you mind," he said.

"All right," said Harry. "Won't go, then. Stay fishin'."

Seeing that this conversation might go on for ever, Cedric decided on direct action. They had tried being reasonable. Harry had had his chance. They would take him by force.

When they came to do it, however, Cedric quickly discovered an error in his tactics: they were on dry land, and Harry was in the middle of the pond. Cedric turned to Andy.

"Get him," he commanded, and pointed in the direction of the pond.

Andy looked from Harry to Cedric, and from Cedric back to Harry.

"He's in the pond," he said, simply.

"Yes," said Cedric sarcastically. "I'm glad you've worked that out all by yourself. The idea, Andy, is for you to get him *out* of the pond."

"I can't. It's wet."

"Of course it's wet, stupid. It wouldn't be a *pond* if it wasn't *wet*. The fish couldn't *swim* in it if it wasn't wet. The general idea is that in order to get Harry, you need to go *in* to the pond where Harry *is*."

Andy took another look at Harry – and the pond.

"But *I'll* get wet if I go in," he protested.

"Tough luck. If we don't *gettim*, we can't *kidnap* 'im, and if we don't *kidnap* 'im, we can't ask for our ransom, can we?"

Andy made a last feeble stand against his leader's authority.

"You go in," he said, weakly.

"I'm the chief. I've got to stay here and *give orders*, haven't I? Who's going to *give orders* if I'm in the pond getting Harry?"

This was all too much for Andy's simple mind. He pulled off his shoes and socks and stepped into the mud. He headed slowly towards Harry, who stood unconcernedly, swirling his stick and swinging his jar.

Andy was not sure what happened next. He took two more steps towards Harry and made a lunge. During the sudden struggle that followed, he received a clonk round the ear with the jam jar. It made his head sing and blow stars. Cedric, trying to help, ducked to avoid a swipe of Harry's big stick and the next orbit of the jam jar. He slipped on the muddy bottom of the pond and fell with a spectacular splash into the water.

There followed an exciting (to Harry) chase in which further damage was inflicted with both jam jar and stick. Also, Andy was bitten in the hand, and Cedric ended up in the pond again.

The scene was witnessed from a safe distance by the

other two Igmopong, Doris Morgan and Amanda Wilson. When it began to look as if Cedric and Andy might lose, they joined in. By the time the seven-year-old battle cruiser was finally arrested, all four Igmopong had received cuts, bruises and various degrees of submersion.

It was at this point, when Cedric tried to get a handkerchief round Harry's mouth, that Harry began to get annoyed. Doris, who had less respect for the social graces, tried pushing a handful of dirt in his mouth, only to have it spat out again into her face.

The Igmopong spent the next several minutes fending off a further supply of punches, kicks and bites. They couldn't hit back at someone of only seven, and were much relieved when the small tornado suddenly subsided.

"Where d'you want to take me?" it said, breathless, and generally happy with the damage to its enemies.

"We're kidnapping you," said Cedric, sucking a wound. "Not that you seem to realise. When you're kidnapped, you're supposed to struggle a bit, and then come. Not kick and punch and *bite* everybody."

"Yes," said the others, examining their injuries.

"We're taking you to our tree-house," Cedric continued, "and we're holding you to ransom."

"Oh, goody!" said Harry, dancing round.

"And you're not supposed to say 'Oh, goody!' either!" complained Doris. She was trying unsuccessfully to wipe away the contents of Harry's mouth from her face and the front of her dress.

Harry's cheerful acceptance of being kidnapped was not what Cedric had expected. In fact, nothing had turned out the way Cedric had expected. A struggle during the actual kidnap was only natural, but not injuries on this scale. And not such an eager victim at the end of it.

"Tie him up," said Cedric. Then, glancing at Harry's changed expression, hastily decided against it. "No," he added, airily. "No. I think he'll come quietly now."

The band of five made its way to the Igmopong tree. Four of them were limping, and one of them was bouncing along, chattily displaying the severely reduced contents of his jam jar. The house stood half way up the tree, ramshackle and precarious. Its floor sloped at a drunken angle because it rested on uneven boughs, and the Igmopong had failed to work out how to keep it level. Its walls were thin, and its roof was two doors tied together with string. The Igmopong were aware that it was not a patch on the Naitabal house. They would do anything to spend a day in the Naitabal tree, and they hoped that the plot to kidnap Harry would achieve just that.

They climbed the rope with some difficulty, mainly because Harry insisted on keeping hold of his jam jar. They finally settled inside. Harry stood at the top end of the sloping floor, and the four Igmopong huddled in a group at the bottom.

Cedric glared at their victim, then took up a bow and arrow. From his pocket he produced the ransom note he had carefully written out indoors. He tied it to the arrow, stood by the window-hole, and took careful aim at the trunk of the Naitabal oak.

"They're all inside," said Charlotte. "I wonder what they'll do now?"

The Naitabals, still squashed together round the south window, had witnessed the kidnapping with great satisfaction. Charlotte, who had lived with her younger brother for all his seven years, knew exactly what would happen.

"They haven't got a chance," she said delightedly, when the battle began. And now that it was over, she said, "I wonder how long they'll want to keep him?"

No sooner had she said these words, than there was a dull thud below them.

"They just fired something," said Jayne. "An arrow."

Toby was at the trap-door, opening it.

"It is an arrow," he said. "It didn't stick in the tree very well. It's on the ground."

Boff helped him to lower the rope ladder, then Toby went down to retrieve the missile. Back inside, the Naitabals gathered in a circle to read the message. It said:

WE'VE GOT HARRY PRISNER

GIVE US YOUR TREE-HOUSE

OR YO'UL NEVER SEE

HARRY AGEN.

SIGNED

CEDRIC MORGAN

From the Naitabal hut came a high-pitched squeal followed by a series of sharp snorts.

It sounded like a pig, but it was the sound of Charlotte laughing.

CHAPTER SIX

Isitor-vung

Mr Blake walked along Meadow Lane, turned left at the Old Corner House where the doctor always lived, along The Avenue, and left again into Brunswick Road. The only thought in his mind was his failing business and how its survival depended on the hidden box of valuable papers.

But why had his cousin been so unhelpful? He could understand her reluctance to dig up her beautiful garden. But when he had suggested using one of those clever diviners which could find things underground, she had seemed afraid.

What was she hiding? Had she already found the box and converted its contents into cash? Or was she hiding something else?

Mr Blake continued along the road and stopped outside Mr Elliott's house. Up on the house front was a sign: E. ELLIOTT, BUILDER. He smiled to himself.

"Just like it used to be fifty years ago!" he thought. "The garden full of rubbish, and the old tree-house built by Eddie's father. And to think we used to play in it with Edith Coates, of all people! Funny how she didn't like being reminded of it . . . "

He sighed a deep sigh, started to climb over the piles of rubbish, and made his way past the skip and down towards the tree-house.

*

"Shall we answer it?" said Charlotte. There were tears in her eyes, and she had stopped laughing at last. "You watch! It won't be long before they beg us to take him back!"

"No," said Ben. "We'll let them sweat it out for a bit."

At last Jayne saw her opportunity to raise a subject that had been intriguing her since she had learned Naitabal language.

"Is someone going to tell me exactly what *Roject-pong Ubmarine-song* is all about?" she said.

"Pigmo watch!" warned Ben.

Charlotte was nearest the south window.

"All clear," she said. "The four of them are still trying to negotiate with Harry!"

"While the Igmopong are so *busy*," said Toby, "it's the perfect time to tell Jayne about it."

"*Show* Jayne about it, you mean," said Ben, winking. "Time to feed the chickens, I think, Boff?"

"Yes," said Boff, grinning back. "But I've made a few changes."

"Starting it was the most dangerous time," Toby put in. "But once we'd done the first bit—"

"Careful, Toby," said Boff. "You'd better stay on watch at the west window – we don't want the Igmopong to hear anything."

Toby stood up and leaned against the west wall.

"Hey!" he said suddenly. "Stranger approaching."

In two seconds all heads were at the west window. A tall, friendly looking but elderly man was making his way towards the tree-house.

"It looks as if he's coming here," said Charlotte. "What do we do?"

"See what he wants," said Ben.

The man disappeared under the Naitabal hut, and five eyes sought spy-holes in the floor to watch what he was doing. He was standing beneath them, face turned up towards them.

"Anybody there?" he called.

"Do we answer?" whispered Charlotte.

"Don't know," whispered Boff. "What does everyone think?"

"No, don't," said Ben, breathing the words as quietly as he could. "If we talk to him he might want to come up."

"We can always say he can't," said Toby.

"*Anybody there*?" called the voice, louder this time.

"Let's face it, he can't come up if we don't let the ladder down," said Charlotte. "Perhaps it'll be OK. He might have something important to say."

"Charlotte might be right," whispered Jayne.

"OK, then," said Ben.

"Who is it?" called Boff in an official sort of voice. "Speak your name and state your business."

"My name is Charles Blake and my business is confidential between yourselves and myself. I wouldn't like all your neighbours to hear it."

"He wants to come up!" said Toby. "Ben was right."

Slowly, they opened the trap-door and five downturned faces looked at the upturned one of Mr Charles Blake.

"What's it about?" said Ben.

Mr Blake whispered as best he could.

"It's about Miss Coates and tree-houses," he said.

Ben spoke sternly, "You'll have to *prove* you're on our side," he said.

"I think I can," said Mr Blake, smiling confidently. He reached into his breast pocket and produced a small rectangle of paper. "You'll need to drop me a line to hang it on," he added.

Charlotte scrambled for a piece of string and it was lowered down. Mr Blake tied a loop at the end of the string, rolled the paper into a tube, and it was hauled up.

It was a photograph. It depicted three children of long

66

ago standing in the doorway of a tree-house. There were two boys with short trousers and hand-knitted striped pullovers, and a girl with blonde hair in a simple dress. They were all bare-footed.

"Is one of them you?" said Charlotte.

"Yes," said Mr Blake.

"It must have been taken a long time ago," said Jayne. Then she suddenly realised what she had said, and how rude it was. "Oh, I'm sorry – I didn't mean . . . "

"That's quite all right," said Mr Blake, still craning his neck towards the trap-door. "It *was* a long time ago."

"It looks a bit like *this* tree," said Charlotte.

"All trees look the same, stupid," said Toby. "Look – it's got branches!"

Mr Blake smiled again.

"Even so – the young lady is quite right – it *is* the same tree!"

"Really?"

"You mean there was a tree-house here before?"

"Oh, yes. Don't you recognise anyone else in the picture?"

"Why should we?" said Ben. "We wouldn't know any of your friends. We don't even know you."

"You know *both* of them," said Mr Blake.

"Someone's grandfather?" suggested Boff.

"Oh, no," said Mr Blake. "The other boy is known to you as Mr Elliott, the builder . . . "

"Wow!" The Naitabals all took a closer look.

"And the girl . . . ?"

Mr Blake smiled and shook his head in amusement.

"The little girl is Edith," he said.

"Edith?"

"We don't know an Edith."

"How about Edith Coates?" said Mr Blake.

There was an awestruck silence as the Naitabals goggled at the photograph. Then they looked at each other.

"*E-wung ould-shong ask-ang im-heng up-ung*," said Ben, slowly. "*Ing ink-thong e's-heng on-ong our-ong ide-song. All-shong e-wung?*"

Mr Blake was suitably confused, but it was one of those occasions when speaking Naitabal was useful. There followed a whispered chorus of *es-yungs*.

Then Ben said to Mr Blake, "The Naitabal hut is top secret, and we *eat* people who give our secrets away."

"I thought you all looked healthy," murmured Mr Blake. "But I do understand. Thank you."

Ben started to unfold the ladder.

"You'd better come up, then," he said.

In the meantime, all was not quiet on Pigmo Island.

When there was no reply to their ransom note, the Igmopong had begun to grow uneasy.

"They definitely found it," said Andy. "I saw Toby Hamilton come down the rope ladder and get it."

"P'r'aps they're thinking up a reply," said Amanda.

"Huh!" said Doris. "And p'r'haps they can't *read*!"

"P'r'aps they don't *wantim* back," said Amanda, darkly. She made an evil face, trying to frighten Harry. "P'r'aps they're gonna leave him here to *die*!"

The four of them looked up the sloping floor at their hostage at the top. As hostages go, he did not seem too worried.

"If they don't come soon," said Doris, trying to join in being nasty, "he'll *starve* to death."

The word "starve" was not a good word to have used. Harry suddenly stopped peering into his jam jar and looked up.

"Hungry *now*." He glared at them crossly. "Want food."

"You're not getting any food until your big sister gives us the key to their tree-house," said Cedric. "So there."

68

Harry ignored this response.

"Hungry," he said. "Want food now."

"Hard luck. You're our prisoner, and you'll piggy well have to wait."

"A few days without food will do you good, anyway," said Doris, who was still smarting from her bruises. "You're too fat."

Unfortunately for the Igmopong, Harry took exception to this personal comment. He stood up and started to swing his jam jar, which the Igmopong had failed to confiscate. He started to advance down the floor towards them. The Igmopong realised, too late, that they had bottled themselves up with a living tornado.

Andy was nearest the rope and went down it at a speed that would have impressed the fire brigade. Doris and Amanda followed, almost burning their hands on the rope. Cedric, still thinking that he could capture the little demon, stood his ground. But only for a second. Although he caught the swinging jam jar in one hand, he also caught the full force of Harry's head in his stomach.

The jam jar, suddenly free, made contact with his elbow. Before it could circle again and make contact with his head, Cedric ducked and dived for the rope.

Harry, unafraid of heights, stood on the plank at the top of the rope, examining the half-empty jam jar. Robbed of their tree-house, the Igmopong re-grouped at the bottom end of the rope, wondering what to do. They stared up at their prisoner.

"Want food – now!" proclaimed Harry.

"Oh, yes?" said Cedric, sarcastically, rubbing his elbow. "Think you're going to get food *now*? After what *you've* done?"

"You're not getting food again, *ever*!" taunted Doris from their safe distance.

Harry stood for a second, like a God, staring down at these little people. They didn't seem to understand who was in charge. They watched, open-mouthed with disbelief, as Harry picked up one of their spears and levered off a piece of the flimsy wooden wall of their precious tree-house. This wasn't an ordinary child of seven they had captured: this was a serpent, a devil, a warmonger, a blackmailer – a criminal genius. He held the small piece aloft, then let it glide down to their feet.

"Want food – *now*," he shouted. The voice itself was a demand.

Cedric looked from the piece of wood to Harry, then to the crestfallen Igmopong. There was another crack of splintering wood from above, and he realised that the tables had been turned. Harry had their tree-house. They did not have Harry. Far from their dreams of possessing Mr Elliott's tree-house – even for a day – they had lost their own. And their problems had only just begun.

"All right," said Cedric. "All right. We'll get you some food. But don't do any more damage."

As they walked dejectedly from the garden into Cedric and Doris's house, a penetrating little voice floated after them, "Bananas an' doughnuts an' licorice allsorts an' ice cream an' . . . "

Mr Blake, having finished his enthusiastic inspection of the hut, sat in a chair. The Naitabals stood against the walls while Jayne stooped down on Pigmo watch. When Jayne had given the all-clear, Mr Blake began to say what was on his mind.

"I think you have a wonderful house here," he said, "and I am honoured to be allowed inside it. Our tree-house was built by Eddie Elliott's father, but it was done in a bit of a rush. As you can see from the photo, not as good as this one."

"Thank you," said Charlotte.

"And now I need your help. I need money – quickly."

70

"We haven't got any money," said Toby, mournfully. "It's no good asking us."

Mr Blake laughed.

"No, no! I don't mean I want money from you!"

He told the Naitabals about his failing business, and the lost box with the valuable papers inside.

"I didn't even know about it until my mother died a couple of weeks ago. So I asked Miss Coates. She said they'd already looked and there was nothing there. But it all seems fishy to me. I can understand her not wanting to dig up her garden to look for it, but when I suggested a diviner – good heavens! She nearly took off!"

The Naitabals exchanged cautious but meaningful glances.

"And now I come back after fifty years," Mr Blake went on, "and see walls and tall hedges round her garden, well . . . I wonder if she's *hiding* something?"

The Naitabals exchanged more glances. They continued to listen, not sure how much they should say.

"And when I was in her garden this afternoon I saw the tree-house. This lovely, magnificent tree-house in the old oak tree where we used to play. And where we used to *spy* on people! I just wondered, you know . . . if any of you had ever seen anything *unusual* going on?"

None of the Naitabals said anything as Mr Blake chatted on.

"That photograph was dug out specially to show to Miss Coates today. I thought it would remind her of the happy times we had together when I used to come here on holiday. But instead of being *pleased* she was *angry* – as if she wasn't the same person – but of course she is. What can have happened in all these years? It's as if she *hates* tree-houses."

"She does," said Ben. "She didn't want this one. She couldn't stop it, but she told Mr Elliott not to put windows overlooking her garden."

Mr Blake laughed.

"No! So you just drilled little peep-holes, I suppose? My cousin must be very stupid not to think of that."

The Naitabals' eyes wandered guiltily to the wall on Miss Coates' side of the hut.

Mr Blake followed them, and smiled.

"What *have* you seen?" he said. "Why is she so *secretive*?"

It was Ben who spoke.

"If we *have* seen anything," he said, "we'd have to have a Naitabal meeting first, to see if we could help."

Mr Blake raised his eyebrows and smiled.

"Well – yes, of course. That sounds hopeful." He stood up. "I must leave you now. But remember – if there's anything I can do in return – *if it's in my power* – I will do it for you! I need to solve this mystery, and you will find that I am a generous man. Thank you."

"You can come back tomorrow morning at ten o'clock," said Ben. "And we'll give you your answer then."

"Thank you, thank you. And now I shall go and call on my old friend Eddie Elliott – if he's in – and give him the surprise of his life!"

Five pairs of Naitabal hands helped to open the trap-door, unfurl the rope ladder and get Mr Blake safely back to terra firma. Five pairs of eyes watched him pick his way over the rubbish and disappear round the side of Mr Elliott's house.

"Wow!" said Ben. "We'll definitely have to feed the chickens now!"

And poor Jayne said, "Will somebody *please* tell me what feeding chickens has to do with *Roject-pong Ubmarine-song*?"

72

CHAPTER SEVEN

Ubmarine-song

"Before we discuss *anything*," said Ben, "Jayne had better be taught how to feed chickens."

"I *know* how to feed chickens," protested Jayne, slightly insulted. "You just stand there with a bucket full of feed, chuck it at them, and they all run around madly going 'brook, brook, brook' trying to be the first to get any."

"Naitabal chickens are a little bit different," said Ben, kindly. "Come on, I'll show you."

"I'll come as well," said Boff. He indicated Charlotte and Toby. "You two can stay on guard."

Boff took a key from a hook on the wall of the Naitabal hut, and two torches from his desk, then he and Ben climbed down the rope ladder and waited at the bottom for Jayne. The three of them walked to the nearby chicken run where Mr Elliott's birds were clucking and scratching. They went into the run and closed the wire gate behind them. Some chickens ran towards them but soon turned back when they saw no bucket.

"You've forgotten to bring the food," said Jayne.

Ben grinned and Boff maintained his calm look of knowing exactly what he was doing.

"Sorry," said Ben, still teasing, "did we say *feed the chickens*? We meant *collect the eggs*, of course."

Jayne, more mystified than ever, followed the boys to the chicken house that stood near the fence by Pigmo

Island. She watched as Boff undid the padlock. The three entered the spacious little hut and Boff closed the door and bolted it from the inside.

It was a solidly built house, designed to last. Made entirely of wood, the floor was covered with straw. All round the sides were nesting compartments where the chickens did their laying, one of them currently occupied by a slightly indignant hen. Another chicken was roosting on one of the elevated perches, making little throaty singing noises. Three lovely eggs nestled in the straw, and Jayne's eyes lit up as she reached out to pick them up.

"Not yet," said Ben. "And make sure you whisper because we're right next to Igmopong territory. If they come too close the others will ring the Naitabal bell."

"Well, we're only getting eggs, aren't we?" whispered Jayne.

"Sshh!" said Boff.

With that, Ben leaned down towards the floor and brushed all the straw to one end where the other two were standing. The rough floorboards ran lengthways along the hut, but Jayne could already make out the shape of a trap-door. Ben pushed a finger into a narrow crevice and pulled. The loose door came away. Ben removed it silently and leaned it against the side wall. Inside the hole was bare earth. Using his hands, Ben scooped the earth away on to the floorboards nearby until he had exposed beneath it another square of wood.

"What is it?" whispered Jayne, but it wasn't much of a question because she already knew the answer. She held her breath as Ben reached down with two hands and removed this new, slightly smaller trap-door to reveal a deep, deep shaft. It seemed as if a rush of cold air came into the hut, but Jayne wasn't sure whether it was that, or herself shivering. She was speechless now.

Ben put a finger to his lips for silence, then showed Jayne how to step down the wood-lined shaft to the bottom. It was exactly a metre and a half deep, and half a metre square. It was possible for the three of them to squeeze in together. Ben took one of the torches from Boff and disappeared from the bottom of the shaft. He had gone, to Jayne's continued amazement, into what was obviously a tunnel. Then Boff switched on the other torch and pulled the wooden cover back into place over their heads so that they were shut inside.

"Now we can whisper again," said Boff. "In case you haven't already guessed, this is *Roject-pong Ubmarine-song*!"

"Oh, submarine! Down below!"

"Follow Ben, and I'll follow you."

"Where does it go?"

"Where do submarines go?"

Jayne frowned in the near-darkness.

"Under the sea . . . "

"You got it!" whispered Boff.

"Not . . . not under the Dreadful Sea . . . !" Jayne's mouth gaped wide.

"Go on, then, or Ben will be at the other end before we've started."

The tunnel was half a metre wide and half a metre high, lined with planks of wood on the floor, walls and ceiling. Every roof section was supported by vertical joists. Jayne crawled forward on hands and knees, lit by the torch that Boff held behind. It was aimed at the shadowy shape of Ben that she could see in the beautifully straight tunnel ahead of her.

"Did Mr Elliott build this, as well?" said Jayne.

"Yes," said Boff. "But we helped. It took nearly six months."

"Where did you get all the wood?"

"Where do you think?"

"Oh, yes. Mr Elliott's yard, of course."

"You mean the Sea of Debris . . . "

"Yes, I forgot."

"Naitabals never forget," whispered Ben from the gloom ahead of them.

They crawled a few more metres. Up ahead, Jayne could see that Ben had stopped and was waiting for them.

"But where did you put all the *earth*?" she said.

"Have a guess."

Jayne thought a bit.

"Not Mr Elliott's skip!"

"Got it in one!"

"But it must have filled it up!"

"It gets emptied every week."

"Do any other grown-ups know about it?"

"Of course not."

"But I don't see how you could have done it without someone suspecting something."

"We'll show you."

None of the Naitabals really knew how long they'd been digging the tunnel. It had become as much a part of Naitabal lore as the tree-house and the islands and the language and the Igmopong. At every opportunity, one of the Naitabals had "disappeared" with Mr Elliott. Another had stayed on watch and two "played" up and down the Sea of Debris in an old wheelbarrow. The first day they did it, they hadn't carried any earth. One or two parents or neighbours had heard the screams of delight, then soon lost interest in just another silly childish game. They didn't carry any earth the second day. But the third day, when they were sure that wheelbarrow rides had become part of everyday life, they had started carrying black plastic sacks of earth at the bottom of the barrow and transporting them to the skip. There they discreetly emptied the contents, which fell out of sight between the bricks and old bits of window frames and broken glass and rubble.

"We're going to dig another one. You can help us."

"Another one! But where does this one go to?"

76

They had reached Ben by now. It was diffcult in the space to turn round, so Ben had straightened his legs and was looking through them back at Jayne, upside down.

"What do you think of it?" he said.

"It's . . . it's just *fantastic*! But where does it go to?"

"It goes to my garden," said Ben, still whispering. He dropped down to his knees again and continued forward. "It's only twenty metres altogether. We've been under the corners of Pigmo Island and the Dreadful Sea, and now we're just about under my shed! Here we are!"

The tunnel had come to an end and Ben was standing up in another shaft. To one side were numerous loose planks, some black dustbin bags and a shovel.

"We left these here for future use," said Ben.

Jayne crawled forward until she could stand up as well. At the top was a square of wood similar to those at the beginning.

"The exit is right in the middle underneath our shed, so the rain never gets in. And you have to crawl on your belly to squeeze out from under the shed. You come out at the back where all the weeds and nettles grow, so no one ever sees you unless you're really unlucky. Even if they did, they'd just say, 'What are you crawling under that shed for?' and you'd just say you were getting a ball out or something and that's the end of it."

Jayne smiled to herself.

"We won't go out now, though," whispered Ben. "No point. Use the shaft to turn yourself round. Boff can turn round in the tunnel, just about."

Jayne did as she was asked, and they began the return journey with Boff in front. When they reached the half-way point, Boff stopped. He pointed his torch into a niche at the side of the tunnel. Jayne caught up and looked. She hadn't noticed the niche the first time because of the dim light and her excitement at everything else. As she looked in, she had another shock.

Boff gave Jayne the torch, then slowly and carefully reached into the niche. Slowly, and very carefully, he pulled out a rusty metal box.

All Jayne could do was gasp.

"We found it when we were digging the tunnel," explained Ben.

Mr Blake had already left the Naitabal oak by the time the Igmopong re-emerged from Cedric's house. They were laden with food taken (illegally) from the kitchen. Jayne, Boff and Ben were already inside the Naitabal tunnel. Nosing from the kitchen window, the Igmopong had seen Mr Blake arrive. Now they were burning to know who he was, and what he had wanted, and what he had sent up on the piece of string.

Even with the Naitabals as sworn enemies, Cedric would normally have wandered over and asked one of the Naitabals jeeringly what did the man want? And why had they invited him into their precious rotten tree-house? And the Naitabals might have told him just as jeeringly to mind his own business. Or they might have told him half the story just to tease him. Or they might have said he wasn't capable of understanding anything properly, anyway. You only had to look at the way he'd built his pathetic tree-house to see that.

But this time it was different. Cedric's gang had kidnapped Harry and had demanded a ransom. To go on over and talk to them now would be to lose face. Once you had started communicating by arrow, you had to keep on communicating by arrow until the affair was settled. He couldn't see much over the fence, and he couldn't go up into the tree-house while that little monster Harry was there. He might be able to see something from the road. He might even meet the stranger coming out.

Sending the others to deliver the plundered food to

78

Harry, Cedric wandered next door into Mr Elliott's front garden. Mr Elliott's van was outside, parked on the hill, so Mr Elliott was home. He looked down the garden at the neat, professionally built Naitabal hut. Not for the first time, he suddenly felt a pang of jealousy. Mr Elliott didn't seem to like Cedric and his friends, but he always let Ben Tuffin and his lot do anything they wanted.

Smarting at the thought, Cedric crept forward over the rubbish. He kept out of sight, trying to see what the Naitabals were doing. He wondered if the stranger was still there. Cedric wished they hadn't kidnapped Harry yet, because then he could just go up and ask them what they were doing, but now he couldn't.

Then it occurred to Cedric that they hadn't answered the ransom note. Its terms had been perfectly clear. Give his gang the keys to the padlock of the Naitabals' treehouse, and the Naitabals could have Harry back . . . But even as he thought of it, it finally began to dawn on Cedric why they *hadn't* answered his ransom note. They knew what Harry was like. They didn't *want* him back.

Cedric sighed and leaned his elbows on the skip, staring down into the rubbish inside it. He wondered how his lieutenants were getting on feeding the little brat. He turned to retrace his steps, but noticed in the skip a heap of paperwork that had obviously been thrown out by Mr Elliott. Some of it looked new. There were letterheads and compliment slips with E. ELLIOTT, BUILDER printed on them, and there was some old correspondence and invoices.

Now Cedric was a magpie. If ever he saw anything that looked as if it might be useful at some time in the future, and it was free, he would take it. Sometimes he would take things that were useless, just because they were free. He reached into the skip and extracted a fat bunch of the stationery.

"This'll do for making notes, an' drawing an' things,"

79

he promised himself, although he had never made a note or drawn anything much in his whole life. Half admitting this to himself, he added, "Well, it'll be useful for *something*, anyway."

And then, as he walked past Mr Elliott's van, an unusual thing happened. Cedric suddenly had an idea. He was not a boy who normally had ideas of his own. Kidnapping Harry had been the result of watching a gangster film on television, not his idea at all. But this idea had come out of the blue. He didn't know how, or why, but it had. There was Mr Elliott's van, here was Mr Elliott's stationery, and there were Ben Tuffin and his lot in Mr Elliott's tree-house. It was so simple, it was unbelievable.

Could he bring it off? Would they fall for it? He ran back to his house and up to his bedroom.

Up in the chicken hut, a fourth egg had now appeared.

"Oh dear," whispered Jayne, "we've shocked that poor chicken into laying."

She was allowed to gather the eggs now, and Ben put his eye to a hole in the outer door and looked up towards the Naitabal hut.

"All clear," he said. He showed Jayne the signal procedure. "If the red flag's at the window, it's dangerous to come out."

Jayne could see there was no red flag. Safely out, they took the eggs and placed them inside Mr Elliott's back porch where they were always placed, then returned to the Naitabal hut for the meeting.

As soon as they were all assembled, with Charlotte on Pigmo watch this time, Jayne started asking questions.

"How did you build the tunnel? How did you get all that earth to the skip? Wasn't it terribly dangerous? If there was a cave-in you could have been *killed*! How did you do it without anyone seeing you? What's in the box?

Why do you leave it down there in the tunnel?"

Boff held up a restraining hand.

"One thing at a time," he protested. "As for building the tunnel, you'll find out very soon. 'Cos we're going to build a branch line, and you'll be doing your share now that you're a Naitabal."

Boff pulled out the drawing he had been making earlier in the day and spread it on the floor.

"You see the *unnel-tong* runs from here, and cuts the corner of the Dreadful Sea? I've worked out if we go off at a right angle *here*" – he indicated the dotted lines on the map – "it's only five metres to the well."

It was the first time any of the other Naitabals had seen Boff's new plan. The air filled with gasps and astonished comments.

"We're going to *tunnel* to the *well*?!"

"Today?"

"On our own?"

"Without Mr Elliott?"

"We can't!"

"What are we supposed to do when we get there?"

"The tunnel might fill with water!"

Boff waved aside the protests.

"I don't know what we're going to do when we get there, but who knows? We might discover something. If it *is* a dummy well, we should go right underneath it, because our tunnel is a whole metre under the surface."

The others considered this in silence, then Boff added, "But it all depends on the box. If Mr Blake will give us anything for the return of the box, I reckon we'd better make use of him before he buzzes off again. Because as soon as he's got it, he'll be off in a flash. He'll be miles away rescuing his business, and he won't be able to do what *we* want."

"What do we want him to do?" asked Ben.

"Ah. You'll have to wait until tomorrow morning for

that," said Boff, mysteriously. "But we mustn't tell him about the tunnel or the well. We'll just say that we have the box hidden. We'll say we found it when we were digging near the SS *Coates*'s fence. OK?"

Everyone nodded agreement, but Jayne was still impatient.

"But what's in the box?" she said. "Is it the one Mr Blake wants?"

"Don't know," said Ben. "The lock's rusty, and we haven't been able to pick it. We didn't want to damage the box, either. We work on it sometimes in the tunnel."

"Break it open!" hissed Jayne, throwing her arms about. "Get a crowbar and *lever* it open! Drop it from a great height and *smash* it open! How can you *stand* not having it open?"

"We've thought about forcing it. But we'd need big tools and a vice. We daren't take it into any of our houses, or we'd be seen with it. So we squirt special oil into the lock every day to loosen it, and try to pick it."

Boff stood up.

"Come on," he said, calling the meeting to an end. "We've got a branch tunnel to dig. If we do exactly what Mr Elliott showed us, it'll be all right."

Through the window, they could all see Pigmo Island. There was no sign of Cedric Morgan, but the other three Igmopong were crouched behind a bush on the far side of their garden. Harry was sitting in the enemy tree-house. Scattered around the tree were empty food wrappers. In Harry's hand was a bow. He was firing arrows towards the bush and shouting that he was Robin 'Ood, and that if they didn't bring him money, he'd come and get them.

CHAPTER EIGHT

Where There's a Well

By half past six Toby was sawing up planks of wood and Jayne and Charlotte were wearing black dustbin bags and giving each other rides up and down the Sea of Debris in Mr Elliott's rusty old wheelbarrow. It wasn't a wheelbarrow, of course, it was a dredger, and the dustbin bags were sou'westers. Toby was standing guard at the Naitabal hut, and Ben and Boff were down in the tunnel. Boff had already measured the tunnel from the chicken end and marked the side planks that needed to be removed to create their branch tunnel to the well.

Boff held the torch now, while Ben struggled to get the pieces of plank away.

"The trouble is," he said, "Mr Elliott did it too well."

They had to move two of the side supports along to free the horizontal plank they supported so that the planks in the wall could be removed. There was not much risk because the ceiling planks were wide enough to be supported by the earth walls. The wall planks added strength and prevented powdered soil from falling in and gradually weakening the tunnel.

As soon as the side planks were out and the roof supports put back, Ben scuttled along to the shed end of the tunnel to fetch the spade. He also collected some of the spare planks left over from their previous efforts, and a small supply of black plastic dustbin bags.

Ben held the torch now, and Boff made the first cuts

83

into the branch tunnel with the spade. He was very careful to do everything exactly the way Mr Elliott had taught them, knowing how dangerous tunnels were. First, four planks were pushed in to form the square section of the new tunnel, supporting the roof and each other. The tunnel was exactly half a metre square, and Toby had already cut planks to the exact measurements they needed. As soon as the planks were firm, the earth from the middle could be safely dug out and shovelled into a black plastic bag. Two bags were needed for each set of planks, and forty planks and twenty bags for each metre of tunnel. They could usually dig a metre of tunnel in a day.

When a bag was ready, it was dragged to the shaft at the chicken hut end. The wheelbarrow would arrive as if by chance, and the bag would disappear as driver and passenger changed places and trundled giggling up the garden again. When there was no one looking, the bag would be emptied into Mr Elliott's skip.

Charlotte changed places with Ben to give him a rest, and by the time dusk was falling the new tunnel was already three quarters of a metre deep. Under cover of darkness, they loaded all the newly cut planks in through the chicken house and down into the tunnel, ready for more work the following morning. The hole was covered up with its door, earth, planks and straw. Thirty bags of earth had been shifted, and everyone was exhausted.

"If we can manage that rate starting at seven o'clock tomorrow morning, we'll have reached the target by twelve o'clock," Ben said, proud of everyone.

"I wonder where Harry is?" said Charlotte, having almost forgotten that her young brother had been absent all afternoon.

Ben, Toby and Charlotte climbed the fence and went to "rescue" him for bed. He was found asleep in the Pigmo tree house, and they had great problems getting him down.

*

At seven o'clock the following morning, Ben and Boff were in the tunnel again. They had with them enough planks to last for two more metres, and enough black plastic bags for all the earth that would be excavated. Mr Elliott hadn't gone out to work yet, and they didn't want anyone using the wheelbarrow so early because it was bound to attract comment or suspicion. There was just enough room in the tunnel to leave bags of earth dotted along its length for later collection. Charlotte had got up early and volunteered to be on watch in the Naitabal oak.

Ben and Boff had only gone forward two more planks in the side tunnel when the spade struck something hard. The two Naitabals looked at each other briefly in the yellow torchlight. Ben, who was holding the spade, leaned further forward and gently explored with the tip, being careful not to make scraping noises. Using their hands as well, they quickly exposed a course of bricks.

"*Ells-heng ells-bang!*" said Ben, using one of his favourite Naitabal expressions. "It's a brick wall, and we're still four metres from the well!"

Boff's eyes glinted with excitement in the cool, dim tunnel.

"I didn't know *what* we might find, but I hadn't reckoned on *this*!"

"What d'you think it is?"

"A wall, silly."

"I can see it's a wall. What for? Why bury a wall?"

"I'm sure they didn't just get a wall and bury it! It must have been built for something! But we'd better get roof planks right up against the bricks first – otherwise we'll have a roof fall. And there'll be a big tell-tale whirlpool of dirt in the Dreadful Sea!"

Together they pushed planks in for support, overlapping them to get the angle they needed.

"There!"

"What's next?" said Ben.

"*Unno-dang*," said Boff. "We could turn the tunnel and go with the wall – but which way, and for how far?"

"I bet there's an underground room! The well must lead right into it!"

Boff was motionless for a second. Then he said:

"I wonder if we could remove a brick – just one – and look inside! Look! The cement is pretty rotten anyway, it's been buried so long. What d'you think?"

Ben hesitated.

"It would show up on the inside. She'd see it."

"Ye – es . . . "

"But if we did it low down we could pack earth against it afterwards. She wouldn't see the tunnel, even if she took the brick out from inside." Ben paused. "But if there's water on the other side it'll flood the tunnel. We'll drown."

"We'd better not do that, then." Boff was worried. "But we can loosen the cement round one brick and make a hole in one corner – just enough to shine a torch in, and not big enough to flood us out."

"She'd still see the hole and be suspicious."

They both thought in silence for some seconds, then Ben suddenly whispered: "I've got it! We can make a small hole, but we'll push a *root* through it afterwards!"

"Brilliant!"

"She'll think it's that tree nearby. We cut through a couple of its roots just now!"

Ben went back to open some of the bags to find a strong-looking root, while Boff started scraping the crumbly cement from around one of the bricks. There was an intense air of excitement in the tunnel, and they were both aware of it.

"I can't get very deep with the spade," said Boff. "It's too awkward. I'll have to have a screwdriver or something."

"I'll get one. There'll be one in the Sea of Debris somewhere."

With that, Ben disappeared towards the chicken end. He was back five minutes later with an iron bar with a point on one end, and a largish rusty drill.

"Everything all right up there?" said Boff.

"Yep. No red flags. Charlotte on watch. No Igmopong. It's eight-fifteen."

"That was good thinking, bringing the drill. It should be easy with that."

Boff moved back and allowed Ben to come forward with the drill. Ben found that he could kneel and still get quite a good pressure on it. He turned the big handle and the bit began to bite slowly into the crumbly cement. After several minutes of patient handle turning, the drill suddenly gave way and they both heard a great hollow thundering noise beyond the wall. It sounded like a huge surf crashing down on a pebbly beach. It was not a healthy sound.

"Oh, no!" said Ben.

Their next impulse was to turn and run – or rather, crawl – away. Then Boff said, "We might as well have a look through the hole while we're here. We've already done the damage."

"But it's only a little hole – less than a centimetre! How can it have made all that noise?"

"Did you feel anything with the drill?"

"I was pushing all the time. It just felt solid, and then it went through."

Ben took the torch with shaking fingers and did his best to peer through the hole.

"I can't get the torch to shine through the hole and my eye to look through it at the same time!" he complained.

Boff tried, with the same result.

"I think we already know what it is. It's an underground room. But we won't be able to see in it from here without doing more damage and raising more suspicion."

"They might think a mole did it," said Ben hopefully.

Suddenly they both wanted to get out. They wanted to be anywhere but there at that moment. They wanted to be somewhere where they could discuss the problem with peace of mind. Quickly, Ben threaded the fattest root he had found into the hole. Together they wedged a plastic bag of earth beneath it and piled earth over the hole. Then they added lots more bags behind until it formed a fairly solid wall that would stand up to any probing from inside the room.

Ben had some lingering doubts that the root might look rather obvious and silly from the other side. But it was nothing compared with the nightmare conjured up by the crashing sound.

"At least I'm sure now," said Boff, "how Mr Blake can help us."

At exactly three minutes to ten o'clock Mr Blake's upright figure could be seen picking its way over the choppy Sea of Debris. At exactly ten o'clock he was settled inside the Naitabal hut, and the pre-arranged meeting began.

"Have you had your discussions, children?" said Mr Blake anxiously.

"Yes," said Boff. "We have."

"And?"

"We think we've found your box."

"You *think* you have?"

"Yes."

"Why do you only think you have? I don't understand."

"What I mean," explained Boff, "is that we *have* found a metal box – buried – just near the fence at the back of Miss Coates's garden down below."

"How did you find it?"

"We were just practising digging, that's all. It was just pure luck that we found it."

"When did you find it?"

"Last June."

"And you still have it?"

"Yes."

"And you think it's the box I am looking for?"

"We don't know. We don't know what's in it."

"Why not?"

"We can't open it."

"It's locked?"

"Yes. And rusted."

"Let me see it."

"No."

"I beg your pardon?"

"No. You can't see it until you've done something for *us* – you promised."

"*If* you found the box, I said – but at the moment there's no evidence to suppose that you have."

"You have to trust us."

"Why?"

"We trusted you when we invited you into our treehouse. It's never been visited by an adult before – except Mr Elliott, who built it."

"Ah, yes! Eddie! I had a nice chat with him yesterday about old times. I do trust you. But why can't I just *see* the box?"

"Because it's hidden."

"Can't you fetch it?"

"No."

"Why not?"

"I've told you. You have to do something for us, first."

"I see. If I refuse?"

"Then you'll never see the box," said Boff, simply.

"All right," smiled Mr Blake. "I'll do whatever I can to

help you. I'm a man of my word – and it doesn't sound as if I have any choice, anyway."

"No."

"And if I do this – thing – for you – what then? When shall I see the box?"

"Tomorrow – maybe."

"Only maybe?"

"It depends what happens. You'll have it as soon as we can get it."

"Very well. I shall be most grateful if it turns out to be the *right* box – *most* grateful. Now – what is it I have to do?"

Mr Blake smiled in anticipation.

Boff hesitated for effect, knowing that he had not discussed his idea with any of the others.

"We want you to take Miss Coates out to dinner tonight," he said. "From eight o'clock until eleven o'clock."

There was a stunned silence and the smile fell from Mr Blake's face.

"That's an awfully long time to be alone with the irascible Miss Coates," he protested. He looked around at the other stunned faces, then back at Boff's determined and serious one. "But, yes. Yes. Is that it? Is that what you want me to do?"

"Yes."

Mr Blake accepted his fate and smiled again.

"So that you can get up to some mischief, no doubt?" he said, with a twinkle in his eye.

"*If we're found out*," said Boff, unwavering, "you'll never *ever* see the box. It's hidden where no one will *ever* find it."

"I – I understand. I understand perfectly."

It was a very thoughtful Mr Blake who sailed out of the Sea of Debris to call on his old friend Mr Elliott again.

CHAPTER NINE

Reachery-tong!

When the Naitabals returned from lunch at half past one, they found an envelope pinned to the trunk of the Naitabal oak. It said, in neat handwriting, "To the children". Inside the envelope was a compliments slip, printed with the words: E. ELLIOTT, BUILDER, and below it was written:

> *I would like to see all five of you together.*
> *Wait by my van. Don't knock. I'll come out*
> *when I see you.*

"It's from Mr Elliott," said Toby. "He wants to see us. It says 'with compliments' after the message, and it's on his proper stationery."

"His van is outside," said Charlotte. "I saw it as I came in."

"Home for lunch," said Jayne.

Boff went up to lock the tree-house. The others went up the garden very slowly, watching the rope ladder disappear inside the Naitabal hut. Boff emerged from the roof and crossed the rope bridge to the oak on Boff Island. Toby crumpled the envelope and the note and threw them into the skip. Boff joined them and they stood by Mr Elliott's van, looking expectantly towards the windows of his house.

They had only been standing there a few moments when there was a strange scraping noise as Mr Elliott's van suddenly started to move forward on the hill. The Naitabals, with their backs to the van, turned when they realised what was happening. They watched helplessly as the van gathered speed. At the same second, while they were looking down the road, there was the sound of shattering glass behind them. They turned to see one of Mr Elliott's house windows collapsing and spraying broken glass in every direction. They turned yet again to see the van careering across the steep hill. It ran half way up the wooded bank on the opposite side of the road and smashed pathetically into a tree.

It was like a bad, bad dream. As the Naitabals stood dumbfounded, Mr Elliott's front door opened and Mr Elliott appeared, covered in dust as usual, looking to see who had broken one of his windows. His look of surprise turned to shock when he saw the Naitabals. It turned to fury when he saw his van.

The Naitabals had never ever seen Mr Elliott in a temper before. But he was certainly in a temper now.

"My van!" he shouted. "And my window! What the hell do you think you're playing at?"

He stormed down the three steps and along the path towards them, shaking his fist. As each foot crashed to the ground, a cloud of dust came off his overalls in great puffs. He looked like a fiery, smoking dragon.

"You've done this, haven't you?" His voice, normally mild and quiet, was powerful and frightening. His nostrils, covered in dust like the rest of him, flared angrily. "Look what you've done to my van, you devils!"

"We didn't do *any*thing!" shouted Charlotte.

He bore down on them and they instinctively backed away.

"Honestly, Mr Elliott! We were just standing here, like you said, and then—"

"Like I said? *Like I said*? What'd'ya mean, *like I said*? I haven't said anything to anyone about touching my van!"

"But you did, sir," said Boff, as politely as he could. "You wrote us a note, asking us to wait by your van."

"Don't give me that!" shouted Mr Elliott. He had passed them now and was marching down the hill towards his crumpled vehicle.

"But – but, sir – " pleaded Boff, "it was on one of your compliment slips! Signed by you! We wouldn't have come if we thought—"

The Naitabals began to follow him at a safe distance, near enough to talk to him, but far enough to run if necessary.

"Signed by me?" Mr Elliott stopped suddenly in the middle of the road and turned on them, shaking a finger. "Don't you come that with me, young 'un." He turned and went on again, striding fast and determined.

"*Honestly*, Mr Elliott. We'll *show* you! – Toby – show Mr Elliott the note."

Toby had stopped, horror-struck.

"I haven't got it!" he said. "I thought we'd finished with it. It was only a note."

"Where is it?" – urgently.

"I threw it in the skip!"

By this time Mr Elliott had reached his van. He was standing, hands on hips and elbows out at his sides, looking down at the damage. He looked up at the scattered group of Naitabals, some turned this way, some turned that, in complete disarray.

"You clear out of my garden!" he shouted. By now, a few neighbours had opened windows and were watching proceedings with interest. Others had wandered outside to see what the commotion was. "*You clear out of my garden – AND MY TREE-HOUSE! NOW! Collect your belongings and GO and give me the keys. NOW. DO – YOU – UNDER – STAND!?*"

*

It was the end of the world. The Naitabals were finished.

First they went back to the skip with tears in their eyes, smarting with the injustice of it all. They scrambled with bare fingers among the sharp masonry, broken glass, splintered wood and rubble (and lots of earth) that filled it, searching desperately for what Toby had thrown away. It was a needle in a haystack – a pebble on the moon. Every time their fingers moved something aside to look beneath it, more earth and sand and brick dust fell into the spaces, burying their slender hopes. It had gone. Fallen down through the spaces like water down a crack. If only they had kept it!

In black despair, they stumbled their way down to the hut. Jayne was openly crying, and Charlotte was doing her best to wipe away pools that insisted on welling up in her eyes. Boff went back through Boff Island – why call it Boff Island now? – and over the rope bridge to re-open the hut. The other four could barely climb the wobbly ladder to go into their headquarters for the last time.

Slowly, dejectedly, they cleared out their belongings. Writing paper, pencils, ruler, whistles, flags, torches, batteries, emergency rations, first-aid kit, blankets – all went out through the gaping trap-door to drop to the ground.

Toby couldn't forgive himself.

"It was *my* fault," he said. "If I hadn't been so *stupid* and thrown that slip away—"

"It's not your fault, Toby. None of us would have thought about keeping it. There was no *reason* to keep it."

"But it's still me that threw it away."

"And we're still Naitabals," said Ben. "We know we didn't do anything to Mr Elliott, so we'll be back."

Toby, still deep in self-disgust, stood staring out of the window. Suddenly, he went down the rope ladder and out towards the road. They saw him again, ferreting in the skip. Then he disappeared. Then he appeared again, looking in the skip. He came back down the garden holding a half brick and a piece of paper.

"He's found it!" said Jayne.

"No." Toby climbed the ladder, handing his finds up to the others. "It was the Igmopong," he said slowly. "Look!" He held out the piece of paper, dirty and rumpled. It was a blank compliment slip. "It was in the skip. They must have found some of them and written the note. So I looked in their front garden." He held up the half brick. It had a long string tied to it. "They must have had this wedged under the wheel of Mr Elliott's van. Do you remember the funny scraping noise just before the van started to move? – A brick on a piece of string – pulled away when we went out and stood by the van. Then the window was smashed to bring Mr Elliott out and make us turn the other way. Then the brick was hauled out of sight!"

"That's brilliant, Toby!" said Boff, and the others agreed.

"It makes me feel better," said Toby. "I had to do *something*!"

"What I can't understand is how Cedric Morgan ever *thought* of it," said Ben. "I mean, normally he's about as bright as a black suede shoe."

The others laughed, and it helped to relieve the tension a bit more.

"And as thick as a whale sandwich," said Charlotte.

"And his IQ has to be measured to two decimal places so it can get into double figures," said Boff.

"And Doris Morgan—"

"And—"

"But, seriously," persisted Ben. "How did he think of it? It was brilliant. You've got to admit it was brilliant. Totally convincing, and perfectly executed. Faultless."

95

"Perhaps we're seeing a new side of Cedric Morgan," said Jayne. "Cedric the Bright."

"Or perhaps it's the only thing he'll do properly all the rest of his life," said Toby.

"But now we've got to work out how to get it back," said Charlotte. "If it's possible."

"Not the way Mr Elliott was talking," said Ben. "I didn't know he could get so angry."

"Have you noticed that the Igmopong are nowhere to be seen?" said Boff. "Hiding away until the heat's died down, no doubt. Cowards!"

"Come on," said Ben. "Let's finish and get out. We can think about the Igmopong later. First, there's tonight! So we'd better put some glue on the SS *Coates*'s peephole covers."

When the Naitabals returned to hand back the keys to Mr Elliott, they found the Igmopong. Cedric and his friends were clustered close to Mr Elliott and his van as sympathetic onlookers.

"Is it *very* badly damaged?" Cedric was saying in a syrupy voice, as Boff approached with the keys.

"Not as bad as I feared," said Mr Elliott. He seemed to have calmed down a lot in the last fifteen minutes.

"If there's anything we can do to *help*, just say," Cedric went on. He and Boff exchanged glances of pure hatred as Boff handed the keys to Mr Elliott. Boff wanted to say, "It really wasn't us, Mr Elliott," but he couldn't bring himself to say it with the Igmopong there, smirking behind his back. He dropped the keys into Mr Elliott's outstretched hand and turned away without a word.

"All four of us could push it back up the *hill*, if that would be any help," Cedric went on, as Boff strode away. "And, of course, we'd *love* to feed your chickens and collect the eggs for you every day like the others *used* to do. It's not far to go, because we only *live* next door . . . "

Boff didn't hear any more.

At five o'clock, when the Naitabals sat dejectedly at the bottom of Boff's garden with their belongings in a pile, their worst fears were confirmed.

Cedric Morgan's head appeared at the open north window of the Naitabal hut. His voice, loud and insulting, cut through their thoughts like a chain saw.

"Mr Elliott says *we* can use his tree-house from now on," he jeered. "He says he doesn't really care *who* uses it, as long as it isn't the sort of people who fiddle with handbrakes and put stones through his window."

The Naitabals pretended not to notice him and endured his taunts in silence.

"You can jolly well build your *own* tree-house now, can't you, if you're so *clever*?"

There was some scuffling and giggling, then the voice came again, "You can use ours if you like. We don't mind. Not that there's much left of it after Charlotte's brother started wrecking it."

Boff got up. He climbed his own oak tree that was a few feet away, and walked on to the wobbly three-rope bridge that connected it with the Naitabal oak. There was one rope to walk like a tightrope, and one rope each side, higher up, for holding under his arms. It was a trip he had done many times, and he went over at speed.

The Igmopong, suddenly shocked into silence, retreated from the window when they saw Boff coming. Now, as he approached at a steady pace, they began to scuttle down the rope ladder like frightened rabbits. They stood in a group at the bottom, cowering and holding each other.

Boff stood on the roof of the Naitabal hut and began to untie the three ropes that had just brought him across.

He threw them across to his own tree one by one. He turned to face the enemy, who were trying to recover some of their dignity.

"Frightened of something?" he said distantly.

"We came down because we thought there might be too much weight on the hut," said Cedric, lamely.

Boff looked down at them contemptuously, then tossed a key in the dust at their feet.

"That's for the chicken house," he said. "You should all be at home with the chickens."

With that, he swung majestically hand over hand down the sloping bough of the Naitabal oak and dropped to the ground. He walked past them back to the road and back into his own garden.

CHAPTER TEN

Well, well, well!

At eight o'clock that evening, Mr Blake escorted Miss Coates to his car and drove her away for dinner in a restaurant some distance away.

At half past eight, under cover of the gathering darkness, the five Naitabals climbed the wall from Boff Island into the Dreadful Sea. They had told their parents that they were spending the night locked safely in the Naitabal hut. Luckily, news of Mr Elliott's ban had not yet reached their homes.

Stealthily, they made their way to the well. They gazed into its secret interior for the first time and saw exactly what Ben had told them was there – several goldfish. They were neatly parked in water which was above the level of the surrounding lawn.

Thanks to Miss Coates's obsession with privacy, the Naitabals were not in danger of being observed from any of the neighbouring houses. Darkness provided even more protection, but there was always the danger that they might be seen from the Naitabal hut. If the Igmopong had the brains to work out what the wooden patches glued on the wall covered up, they were in trouble. That was a risk they would have to take.

After their initial look, Toby, Jayne and Boff went to various vantage points to act as look-out for prowlers in the adjacent gardens. Ben and Charlotte stayed at the well to try to solve its mystery.

"What did Miss Coates do *exactly*?" whispered Charlotte.

"She took the bucket out."

"Let's do that, then."

Charlotte held the torch while Ben manhandled the bucket off its hook, being careful not to bump it and make a noise.

"Then what did she do?"

"She fiddled with ropes or something. I don't know what. She just fiddled."

They both peered into the shaft again. The wall of the well was a metre high, and the surface of the water inside was about sixty centimetres down. On top of the wall were two thick wooden supports which held up a wooden tiled roof. Inside the roof, high up, was a spindle wrapped with rope, connected to a handle lower down on one of the supports.

"There isn't anything to fiddle with," concluded Charlotte.

"I'm sure she might have been leaning into the well while she was fiddling . . . " said Ben, uncertainly. He frowned, rolled up one sleeve, put his hand into the cold water and felt around. There were slimy weeds, pebbles, and larger rocks, but then his fingers closed on what felt like a chain. He pulled it upwards and it slid through his fingers until he held one end out of the water. It was attached to the inside of the fish pool at one edge under the water. On the end that he held was a large ring.

Excited, Ben leaned further over and searched under the water again. He found another chain, and another, then a fourth. They were evenly spaced around the rim of the tank, and they all ended with a ring.

As Ben was doing this, Charlotte had started working things out. She was currently shining the torch up into the roof space. She discovered that by unwinding the handle attached to the bucket rope, the hook dropped down. Ben

100

hooked the four rings on to it one by one, then Charlotte took up the slack.

"Wow!" he whispered, and Charlotte grinned in the near-darkness.

Charlotte kept hold of the handle while Ben rounded up the other three Naitabals. They gathered round eagerly to see what Ben and Charlotte had discovered.

Five heads looked into the well as Charlotte cranked the handle. The four chains tightened, then suddenly the edge of the water, which they could now see was under a circular rubber skirt, started to rise in the air!

"I don't believe it!" hissed Toby.

The rubber skirt rose up and fell back as the metal rim of the water container went past it. Dish, fish and water were rising out of the well, suspended on the end of the bucket rope!

Charlotte continued to wind until the container had disappeared completely into the roof. By pulling a special hook across, she fixed the handle into position.

No one had dared put their head under the rising fish tank in case Charlotte had let go of the handle, but now five heads craned over the side and looked into the hole.

Miss Coates leaned back in Mr Blake's nice comfortable company car.

"I must say it's very thoughtful of you to take me to dinner this evening," said Miss Coates, when they were fifteen minutes into their journey. "But, you know, I'm not a big eater, and I would much rather we had a light meal somewhere local. I have a slight headache, I'm afraid. There seems to have been too much excitement in the last few days."

"Once you've settled into where we're going, I'm sure the headache will go. What you need is a nice relaxing drink or two."

"Yes, you put me under a lot of pressure when you asked about the buried box – and I'm *very* thankful that you haven't brought the subject up for a whole day."

Mr Blake smiled graciously in the oncoming headlights. "Don't mention it."

"Now," Miss Coates went on, "far be it for me to discourage an old friend and cousin I haven't seen in fifty years, but I now find myself asking the question: what are you waiting for, Charles?"

Mr Blake was slightly taken aback and stirred uneasily in his seat. All he could do for the moment was to repeat the question. "What am I waiting for?"

"Yes, Charles. You haven't mentioned the box for a whole day. That means you've given up, or you hope I'll change my mind. Either that, or you've invited a gaggle of metal-detecting, box-divining experts to come and give my garden a medical."

"None of those things, Edith," said Mr Blake hastily, then realised that he had fallen into her trap.

"You mean you haven't given up, you don't hope I'll change my mind, and you've no plans to get my garden divined?"

"No. No, I don't mean it like that . . . "

"Well, have you given up, or haven't you?"

"No, I haven't. I need that box as much as I did before."

"Then I'll go back to my original question: What are you waiting for?"

Mr Blake, thoroughly confused, repeated the question again, trying to get more thinking time. "What am I waiting for?"

"Don't keep repeating the question, Charles. It's no use waiting for me to change my mind about digging up the garden, because I won't. And I certainly won't allow any so-called specialists in my garden. *So what are you waiting for? Why are you still here?*"

Somehow – he didn't know how – Mr Blake had got himself cornered. And he wasn't sure that he could see his way out. He started to stutter.

"I – I hoped—" he began, then faltered and stopped. He couldn't tell her the real truth: that he'd more or less given up because he hoped the box had been found. What the children were up to, he hadn't the least idea, but that wasn't his problem. As he struggled with his reply, Miss Coates suddenly sat bolt upright in her seat.

"Charles!" she yapped. "I know what you're doing!"

"Y-you do?" stammered Mr Blake.

"Yes! You've arranged for your metal-detectors and diviners to come this evening – *and you're taking me out to dinner to get rid of me while they do it – aren't you*?"

"No, Edith, of course not! That's complete nonsense!"

"I don't believe you! The *only* reason you've been quiet today is because you thought you'd got the problem solved already! I know what businessmen are like when they're desperate for money. They'll do *anything*! Any mean trick in the book!"

"But, Edith—"

"Take me back, Charles! *Turn this car round and take me back!*"

Cedric Morgan sat in the Naitabal hut eating sweets, drinking lemonade and reading comics by torchlight. His sister Doris and the other two Igmopong had decided to stay indoors (they were afraid of the dark). Cedric, however, had been unable to resist being inside his new tree-house during the first exotic hours of darkness. He finished his last sweet, finished his last comic, had his last swig of lemonade, then switched off his torch. He was tired. He closed his eyes and half-dozed for a little while, dreaming nice dreams of victory and cunning. A few minutes later he recovered and got up to look through the windows at the dark and mysterious gardens. He looked out of each of the three windows in turn, finding little of interest because he couldn't see much. Then he idly shone his torch on the fourth, windowless wall. The light picked out the little squares of wood that were stuck on it at intervals.

"I wonder what those are for?" he said aloud to himself.

Having nothing else to do, he took out his penknife and started levering off one of the little squares.

"Look at that!" hissed Ben.

The Naitabals were all looking down the well with their eyes popping out of their heads. The shaft was two and a half metres deep, and at the bottom was not water, but a concrete floor. What made them gasp more than anything was the gap in one side of the vertical inside wall: because through the gap they could just make out a doorway.

They had solved part one of the Mysterious Sinking of the SS *Coates*!

The Naitabals raised their heads for a moment and looked at each other in astonishment.

"Wow!"

"Should we all go down?" whispered Charlotte.

"No," said Ben. "I'll go down first and see if I can get in. I'll call you if it's OK."

Eager hands helped him over the side. He went down using the iron rungs that ran down inside the well. Even before he reached the bottom he whispered excitedly, "There's a key in the door! You can come down!"

There wasn't going to be room for all of them at the bottom of the shaft together, so Ben turned the key and pushed the heavy oak door inwards. He flashed his torch into the secret underground room that gaped before him, and straightaway had his first shock.

"Oh no!"

The others were following down in quick succession now, and Boff brought up the rear.

"Try putting that light on," said Ben.

Boff did so, and the little room flooded with light.

It was just before nine o'clock when Mr Blake's car drew up outside Miss Coates's house. Miss Coates scrambled to get out of it.

"If I find any of your people in my garden . . . !" She left the threat unfinished, and was gone.

Mr Blake remained sitting in his car. He'd thought of pretending to run out of petrol, having a puncture, or getting lost, but his cousin was no fool. None of those ploys would have delayed them more than a few minutes. He didn't know what to do. He'd let the children down. He knew they were up to *some*thing, but he didn't know what – and now he'd dropped them in it, as the expression was. His chances of ever seeing the legendary box were just about zero.

His thoughts were interrupted by the return of his cousin. Her voice, previously angry and sharp, was now sweet and apologetic.

"Charles! I'm so sorry for doubting you. I've been such a fool! Of course there's no one in the garden, and I've been an ungrateful wretch and ruined your evening for you. I feel so *bad*!"

Inside, Mr Blake breathed a sigh of relief.

"I *told* you—" he began, but his cousin interrupted.

"Come into the house," she said, "and I'll get you a lovely supper."

"Can't we just go out?" said Mr Blake, still nervously trying to get her away from the house for the children's sake. "I need a drink."

"I've got drinks in the house," said Miss Coates.

Mr Blake hesitated, but only for a second. Better to be

where he could at least keep an eye on her, he thought.

"All right," he said. "I'll come in."

They went into the house. Miss Coates settled her cousin in the sitting room with a large drink. Then she went up to her bedroom to freshen herself up after the rather traumatic car ride. Her bedroom window overlooked the garden, and she always drew the curtains at night before switching the light on. But now, in what was supposed to be the darkness of her garden, she noticed a funny, faint glow.

She immediately picked up the strong poker she always kept for protection by her bed, and a torch. Then, without disturbing her cousin, she crept downstairs and out into the garden.

The Naitabals were standing in a little room nearly four metres long and less than three metres wide. Along each side of the room were wide benches. The walls were white, plastered, and crumbling. At the far end on the floor was an electric radiator with a red light glowing. On the three walls hung five magnificent paintings in gold ornate frames.

"Close the door!" said Ben.

Boff closed it, and they all stared again at the thing that had made them gasp with horror. Where Ben's root stuck out of the wall, a huge area of plaster had fallen off, exposing the red bricks. Big pieces of plaster were scattered all over the left-hand bench and across the floor.

The damage they had done with the drill was so blatant that none of them knew what to say.

"It doesn't *really* look as if the root could have done it, does it?" said Ben at last. "In fact, it's pathetic."

"Perhaps we should cut it off while we're here. We can shove some plaster in the hole. The plaster's so bad, it could have fallen off by itself, anyway."

"The damp's coming through from the earth. That's why the cement was so crumbly."

Charlotte was looking at the pictures.

"I wonder why someone would want to keep five such beautiful pictures all by themselves in an underground place like this?" she said. "It doesn't make sense."

They all looked at the pictures. Two of them were landscapes, one was a portrait, one an abstract, and one was of flowers.

"Why go to all this trouble for five paintings?" said Charlotte again. "Is she afraid of burglars, or something?"

At this moment they all heard a noise behind them and froze. Together, slowly, they turned.

Standing in the doorway, with a torch in one hand, and a poker in the other, was the SS *Coates*.

CHAPTER ELEVEN

Rapped-tong

Miss Coates closed the door and stood with her back to it, staring at the horrified faces of the children in front of her. Her own shocked expression travelled from the Naitabals to the huge patch of brickwork exposed by the fallen plaster, then to the paintings on the walls.

The Naitabals didn't know quite what to make of her. She didn't immediately explode as they might have expected. She was like a firework whose fuse had fizzled out: they were afraid to disturb her in case she suddenly went off.

The seconds passed. No one said anything.

Then, gradually, Miss Coates started to tremble. Was she cold, or was it the beginning of a massive Coatesanic eruption? The Naitabals were expecting her to call them Wicked, Wicked Children, and to rant and rave and scream and wave her poker at them. They squeezed closer together for protection, expecting the worst. But no onslaught came. Instead, the SS *Coates* looked round the group once more. She spoke, not in her usual ship-to-shore foghorn sort of voice that they were used to, but quietly, like a little mouse: "Oh, children, you *naughty* children . . . What *am* I going to do? What *am* I going to do with you?"

But even before the Naitabals had time to think what the SS *Coates* was going to do, there was an unexpected disturbance behind her. The first sound was that of the key being turned in the lock from outside. Miss Coates swung on her heel, but too late: the door was solidly shut. Then, mixed in with the clatter of hurriedly climbing footsteps, came the small but distinct voice of Cedric Morgan.

"That'll teach *you* to go sneaking about in other people's gardens, *Ben Tuffin* and you *others*!"

By the time Miss Coates had regained control of herself, realised what was happening, and shouted, "Unlock this door, you ruffian!" in her strongest voice, the footsteps had already subsided across the lawn above their heads. Further shouts were to no avail.

"That was Cedric Morgan," said Ben. "Has he locked us in, Miss Coates?"

Miss Coates nodded. Then, sighing heavily, she sat down on the bench by the door.

"Well," she said. "It looks as though we're stuck here, doesn't it?"

"We're very *very* sorry, Miss Coates . . . " began Ben falteringly, "about being here in your – in your garden. We . . . we didn't mean any harm, and . . . "

"Well, you might as well all sit down instead of standing there goggling at me like a lot of half-wits," said Miss Coates. This mild-mannered lady certainly wasn't the fiery old dragon they were used to.

A great deal of shuffling and scuffling went on before the Naitabals were finally settled on the benches as far away as possible from their unpredictable enemy. They still treated her as if she were a hairy spider that might leap up and bite their heads off and suck the juice out of them.

"As we might be here for some time," said Miss Coates, "perhaps your friends had better introduce themselves?" She added that all the faces were familiar, and that she had probably heard their *voices* on *many* occasions.

"I'm Charlotte Maddison."

"Jayne Croft."

"Toby Hamilton."

"Barry Offord."

"His friends call him Boff," Ben explained. "Because he can be a bit of a boffin sometimes."

Boff smiled self-consciously.

"Only because my dad helps me," he said. "He's an engineer."

"And I suppose that as soon as you all escape from here you'll be telling the whole neighbourhood what you've seen?"

"No, Miss Coates," said Ben.

"No?"

"No, Miss Coates. We're Naitabals, and Naitabals can keep a secret."

"You're *what*?"

"Naitabals, Miss Coates."

"And what exactly is a Nay-ter-bull?"

"A cross between a native and a cannibal, Miss."

"I see." Miss Coates was quietly intrigued. "And how do I know that – Naitabals – can keep a secret?"

"We've already got some that no one knows about," said Ben. "If any of us told a secret, we'd be driven out of the Naitabals for ever. That's why" – mysteriously – "we only take certain types of children. Cedric Morgan could never be a Naitabal in six thousand seven hundred years."

"The boy who locked us in?"

"Yes."

"If that's the case, you're saying *he's* the sort who *will* tell everyone in the neighbourhood what he's seen . . ."

"Probably," said Ben.

"*Definitely*," said Charlotte.

"Oh, dear," said Miss Coates, keeping her voice low in case anyone outside might be listening. "That's the *last* thing I wanted. I have kept *my* secret for over forty years, and now it's all going to be spoilt because of you naughty, naughty children."

"We won't spoil it." To the others: "Will we?"

The others shook their heads fervently that they wouldn't.

"Honestly we won't. We know how exciting it must be to have a secret underground room like this."

"How did you discover it?" Miss Coates indicated the room with a sweep of her hand. She had recovered herself now, but she still wasn't looking angry. Her voice was almost soothing, nothing like the sharp penetrating shrill they were used to.

It was this that made Ben tell her (most of) the story from beginning to end. How he had seen her going down the well, how he had crossed her garden to look into it, and how they had waited for her to go out before having a proper look. He didn't mention the deal with Mr Blake, or the tunnel that ran under the corner of her garden, or how the plaster had come off her wall.

Miss Coates smiled from time to time, and when Ben had finished, she gave a great sigh.

"So!" she said. "Just silly childish curiosity. And after all my careful planning . . . Well, your curiosity has killed the cat, my dears. The secret I have kept since after the war will now become public knowledge. Unless I *murder* you all, of course. But then I'd have to murder Cedric Morgan and all of *his* gang before morning as well, I suppose. No. No, that won't do. That won't do at all, will it?"

The Naitabals agreed that it wouldn't.

"Perhaps that root coming through the wall up there and knocking all the plaster off the wall is my final warning," she added, looking up to where the huge patch of brickwork was showing.

Ben and Boff exchanged brief glances of relief and congratulation.

"What do you mean, a warning?" said Charlotte.

"It's been getting damper and damper over the years. I've had to spend more time down here keeping everything clean and dry. Now the root coming through has shown me just how bad the walls and the plaster are. It seems to be telling me it was time I abandoned the room and solved the problem some other way."

"What problem, Miss Coates?" said Jayne.

Miss Coates heaved an enormous sigh.

"What's the room for?"

"Why's it so secret?"

"Well," said Miss Coates, "I suppose you'll have to know. It looks as if we're all locked in here for a while until that silly boy decides you've had enough. I'm sure he wouldn't have dared do it if he'd realised I was here as well. So we might as well pass the time with a story."

Miss Coates made herself a little more comfortable on the bench, as much as the hard wood would allow.

"Do your parents expect you back at any particular time?"

"We told them all we were staying together in the Nait-abal hut," said Ben.

"The Naitabal hut?"

"Sorry. Mr Elliott's tree-house."

"Isn't that dangerous?"

"No. We padlock ourselves in."

"Except that we haven't got it any more," said Charlotte. "So we had to lie about that bit." Then she added hastily, "Naitabals only tell lies when it's *absolutely* necessary."

"Why haven't you got it any more?"

Briefly, Ben told her about the nasty trick that Cedric Morgan had played on them and Mr Elliott.

"I think," said Miss Coates when he had finished, "I'm beginning to dislike this Cedric Morgan more and more. He almost makes *you* look *normal*, Ben Tuffin."

It was the first kind thing that Miss Coates had ever said to Ben since he could remember. He blushed. Perhaps she wasn't such an old battleship after all.

"Well. Time for my story," said the battleship. "Do any of you children know what we're sitting in?"

"A secret underground room," said Ben.

"Yes – but what *is* it – or *was* it?"

"I don't know."

"It was built during the war as an air-raid shelter. A lot of houses had them. This one had a much larger opening where the well is now, with steps going down to it. When there was a bombing raid and the sirens went off, we could always come down here and be a bit safer from flying glass and fire and falling bricks."

"It must have been fun!" said Charlotte.

"It *was* great fun at first. Then it became rather tiresome. Having to get out of a warm bed in the dark and traipse out into the cold night. And lying on a hard bunk bed was no joke once the novelty had worn off, I can assure you."

"We'd love it, wouldn't we?" said Jayne.

"You bet!"

"Then the war ended. And *that* was when my father took up his new occupation."

"What was it?" said Jayne.

"What I am going to tell you is *absolutely secret*," said Miss Coates. She looked carefully at the faces bunched together at the far end of the shelter. She seemed to be making a decision. Then she added, "I'll *have to* trust you. But it's so secret, it's the *very thing* I've been successfully hiding all these years – until now. And now I can't see any way out. Do you all solemnly *swear* that you will never breathe a word of this to *anyone*, as long as I shall live?"

She made each of the Naitabals solemnly swear in turn, then she breathed another deep sigh and made her statement.

"My father," she said quietly, "was a burglar."

There was a gasp from the Naitabals.

"Your *father*?"

113

"He couldn't be!"

"A *burglar*?"

"Not an *ordinary* burglar," she hastened to tell them. "He was a very exceptional *high-class* burglar."

"What do you mean, a high-class burglar?" said Toby. "Was he royalty or something?"

"No, no. I mean, he only burgled exceptionally fine things. He was a fine art thief. The *only* thing he burgled was paintings."

Slowly, the Naitabals' eyes swivelled to the paintings on the walls.

"Yes," said Miss Coates. "Those are my secret. I had to hide them in case I died and someone found them in the house. My parents died in a car crash soon after the war. I inherited the house, of course. When I went through my father's papers I unlocked the room in the house that he always kept to himself. That was when I found out – and found these." She swept her hand around the walls at the five paintings. "Do you know how much they are worth?"

The Naitabals did not dare to guess.

"I'll tell you. If we were able to sell these five paintings on the open market today, and split the money between the six of us, we would all be millionaires."

This time several mouths dropped open and there were more gasps of disbelief.

"*Millionaires*?"

"Oh, yes. The Picasso is worth over two million, the Rubens a similar figure, the Turner quite a lot, the Monet over two million, and the Renoir over three million."

"Well, why don't you sell them, then?" said Boff. It seemed the logical thing to do.

"One, they're not mine. Two, they can't be sold on the open market – they're stolen and very famous. Three – and most important – I don't want *anyone* to know that my father was a burglar. As far as I know, these are the only paintings he stole. He must have been at the beginning of his career in crime, building up a portfolio of works. Next, he would be trying to find clients who would pay a lot of money on the black market. The paintings would go into their private, secret collections. There are plenty of crazy, crooked millionaires in the world. They want a certain painting and they'll pay anything to get it."

"Why didn't you *give* them back?"

"Because *I didn't want anyone to know that my father was a burglar*. I couldn't bear the thought of being seen as the daughter of a crook – because that's what my father was – no more, no less."

"So why didn't you *send* them back?" said Toby.

"You'll think me silly, I know, but I didn't send them back because I didn't know where they came from. I didn't have the *courage* to ask about them without raising suspicions. I'm sure I could have spent a day in London casually talking to art experts, but I just decided to *hide* them where no one could possibly find them – perhaps until I *heard* something about them, or read something. I put quick-growing hedges round the garden, encouraged tall trees and then – *finally I built the well* – myself – when I was sure no one could see what I was doing.

"The next stage, when I'd locked them safely away, was loving them. I'd had them so long by now, I couldn't bear to part with them. I'd go down the well at least once a month in the small hours and sit here in front of them. *Renoir* painted that, I would say to myself, or, it was *Rubens'* hand created that. I was as bad as the mad millionaires they were stolen for in the first place. But now – now I realise it couldn't last for ever. And if I'd died they would have rotted down here and been lost for ever. So I'm *glad* my secret is out. I've been lucky to keep it for forty years – but now we must think of a way to protect me. Whatever happens – and you're all *sworn* to secrecy – the family name of Coates must be protected."

"We'll help – we'll do anything we can," said Charlotte earnestly.

"We're Naitabals," said Jayne. "Naitabals can do anything."

"We'll take 'em back," said Toby, bold as anything. "Won't we?"

"Yes. We'll take 'em back."

"No one'll notice if it's just children."

"If only it were that simple," said Miss Coates. "Who do they belong to, that's the question? If insurance money was paid out, the pictures might belong to the insurance companies. Or, if not, the owners might have died, and they belong to someone else in the family, or a charity – or public galleries. It's so complicated! But before we can do *anything*, we've got to get out of here. I hope that stupid Cedric Morgan boy isn't going to leave us here all night. *And how do we stop him telling anyone else about this room*?"

While Miss Coates had been talking, Ben had been thinking. His face was beginning to light up.

"I know how," he said. "I know how we can do *everything*. Get the paintings back. Protect your name, *and* stop Cedric talking. As long as he's the only one who *saw* anything. It doesn't matter if he *tells* the other Igmopong, as long as they don't *see* anything. Then we can do it."

"It sounds like a miracle to me," said Miss Coates, "but who are the Igmo . . . er . . . pong?"

"Cedric Morgan's gang," said someone.

"Oh, I see. Yes. And exactly how do you propose to do all this, Ben Tuffin?"

Ben leaned forward on the bench.

"We've got to get out of here first, of course," he said, "*before* Cedric Morgan comes to let us out."

"This is an oak door, Ben. Even with this poker I brought along to crack you snoopers on the head, we couldn't break the lock on that door."

"There's another way," said Ben.

CHAPTER TWELVE

Lans-pong

"No there isn't," said Miss Coates. "The door is the only way out."

Ben looked briefly at the other Naitabals. They already knew what he was thinking, but he needed their support.

"It means giving away a Naitabal secret," he said, "an' Naitabal secrets are even more secret than government ones."

"But if all Naitabals agree," said Boff, "that something's absolutely necessary . . . "

The other Naitabal heads nodded in agreement.

"Anyway," Ben went on, turning to Miss Coates, "you've given us a very valuable secret of yours and we've all sworn to keep it, so it's only fair if we give you a valuable secret of ours. But *you* must swear to keep it as well."

Miss Coates, freed of her guilty conscience, was beginning to enjoy herself. She hadn't had so much excitement in one night since she was ten herself, having midnight feasts in the tree-house – *yes, the tree-house*. Hiding all the food under the bed and sneaking it into the tree at twelve o'clock . . .

"Of course I will," she said.

"Repeat after me," said Ben. "I promise absolutely on pain of death . . . "

"I promise absolutely," – Miss Coates took a deep

breath and spoke the alien words self-consciously – "on pain of death . . . "

"Never to reveal to any living soul . . . "

"Never to reveal to any living soul . . . "

" . . . the secret of the *Roject-pong Ubmarine-song*."

" . . . the secret of the Roj – ect – pong – Ub – marine – song, er, what is that, children?"

"That means," said Ben sternly, "that you can't even tell my father about it – and you've sworn on pain of death."

"Which means," said Toby, making everything perfectly clear, "that if you tell anyone, we'll have to put you to a horrible death and eat you."

"'Cos we're cannibals."

"Oh, dear."

"And now I'll tell you what *Roject-pong Ubmarine-song* is."

"I'm so pleased."

"It's a tunnel."

Miss Coates's face, which had already taken on a strange, unreal sort of look, stiffened to something of the old face they were used to.

"A *what*?!"

"A tunnel," said Ben.

"*Where* is this tunnel?"

"It goes from the chicken house in Mr Elliott's garden to underneath the shed in my garden."

"Just a *minute*!" cried Miss Coates. "*My garden* is in between those two places!"

"Yes. I'm afraid we had to go under your garden in the corner."

"Good gracious!" cried Miss Coates.

Ben enlightened her further. "And that piece of root sticking out of your wall isn't a natural piece of root" – all eyes travelled to the scene of destruction – "I mean, it is a piece of *root*, but it didn't get there natural. Naturally, I mean."

"How did it get there, then?"

"It's where our *new* tunnel finishes," said Ben.

"Well, frogs in my pond and larks singing above!" cried Miss Coates.

The Naitabals noted this expression for future use. Then Ben explained how the tunnel had been extended to solve the mystery of the well.

"I think," said Ben, "that if we used your poker, we could all get out through the tunnel."

Cedric Morgan sat on his bed, breathless with suppressed excitement. Doris was asleep, so he couldn't tell her he had seen Ben Tuffin and his silly old gang disappearing down the well in Miss Coates's garden. And it was too late to call on Andy and Amanda, and he daren't risk using the telephone in case any grown-ups overheard, or wanted to know what was going on. It was so frustrating! He couldn't tell *anyone* that he had seen those dopes through the spy-holes in the tree-house wall, thinking they were so clever and better than anybody else! He savoured the moments when, seeing the last member disappear into the well, he had descended the rope ladder more quietly than any old Tarzan could have done, climbed Miss Coates's back fence like a stealthy panther, then crept over to look down the well. And when he realised they were inside that door, and all he had to do was turn the key and run . . . !

He had bounced up and down on his bed with glee until his father had come in and asked him what all the jumping was about, and he had said Nothing, what jumping? And now, realising that he had to keep his wonderful secret bottled up inside for the whole night, he decided what he would do. Ben Tuffin and his rubbish friends could stew in that place *all night*, and in the morning he would go round to Miss Coates's house with the key which he'd taken. He'd say he'd seen some boys going down her well last night, and did she think she'd like to have a look? And then she'd go and have a look, and find them, and they'd all be in big, big trouble!

Oh, he was busting for the morning to come! Busting, busting, busting!

Mr Blake finished the drink that his cousin had so kindly given him, and waited for her to come downstairs to keep him company. Everything seemed to have gone incredibly quiet. He began to wonder if she was all right. He thought at one point that he heard her coming downstairs again, but she hadn't been upstairs long enough to change, then. Perhaps something had happened to her. Perhaps she was feeling ill and was too weak to call for help . . .

He raised himself from the nice comfortable chair and went to the bottom of the stairs.

"Edith!"

No answer. He went halfway up the stairs and called, louder.

"*Edith!*"

Still no answer. He carried on up the stairs to the upper landing. All the doors were ajar. He knocked on each in turn, calling her name, then looked inside each one. Nowhere to be seen.

He went downstairs again and did the same thing, calling all the time. The front door was bolted on the inside. The back door was closed, but not locked. Mr Blake went outside. The air was cool and it was pitch dark. He found a torch, went outside again. He walked round the garden, flashing the torch. The light fell on the well. She couldn't have fallen down that. He'd seen it the day before. It was one of those dummy things with goldfish moping around inside it. If she'd fallen into it, he'd be able to see her feet sticking out of it a mile off.

"Strange!" he muttered to himself, giving up the search.

He went back to the sitting room, called her name once more, then poured himself another drink.

"Must have popped into a neighbour's," he concluded, settling down.

Ben told them all his plan of action, received due applause, and set them to work. They took it in turns to scrape at the crumbly mortar around the bricks to try to work them loose.

"Don't make too much noise, children – no banging," warned Miss Coates. "We mustn't let anyone *else* suspect that there's anything down here, or questions will be asked!"

"They'll just think we're a big mole," said Charlotte.

They set to work, first Ben, then Miss Coates, then Toby, then Jayne, Boff and Charlotte – all digging, scraping, cutting the lines of cement with the sharp end of the long poker. Once the root was cut off and pushed back through the wall, each of them tried to get the point of the poker into Ben's drill hole to lever the first brick out.

It was hard work. Before long they were all perspiring and grunting with each new effort, and the air in the little room was getting stale. Miss Coates, whose previously pale and powdered cheeks were now pink and shiny, switched on an extractor fan.

"That'll help," she said. "I must say, we're very fortunate this mortar is as crumbly as it is. Otherwise we would have needed a hammer and chisel."

At last the first brick came out and fell with a thump on the wooden bench, followed by a long trickle of earth, running like a waterfall, spilling out of the hole on to the bench and the floor. Cool, fresh air blew into their faces.

It had taken longer than any of them expected. Even when one brick was free, the others were still hard work. Gradually, two, three and four bricks were loosened, and there was a pile of earth, bricks and cement dust. At last they could reach into the dark tunnel and pull out the black plastic bags of earth that had been used by Ben and Boff to wedge against the pile of earth next to the bricks in the tunnel.

They had to remove seventeen bricks altogether. An hour and a half had passed and they were all exhausted. Miss Coates, having voiced a warning about the dangers of tunnels, was nevertheless impressed by its wooden lining and supports. The tunnel was only just wide enough for her shoulders, and it was not going to be easy getting her through.

But they did get her through. Toby went first, then Jayne, then Miss Coates, squeezed in with great encouragement and help from the others, followed by Charlotte, Boff and Ben. It was a strange procession in the torch-light, six people on their hands and knees, especially the grown-up in the middle in her pretty cocktail dress. They quietly puffed, panted and slithered their way along the planks towards Ben's garden. Ben remembered to collect the box from its hiding place in the tunnel wall.

Toby stood up when he reached the shaft. He stretched above his head, pushed up the trap-door and lifted it to one side, out of sight under Ben's garden shed. Then he hoisted himself up and wriggled on his tummy over the dry earth. He kept his head down as he emerged under the rear edge of the shed among the weeds and long grass. For the other children it was quite easy, all of them except Jayne having had plenty of practice. For Miss Coates it was not going to be easy at all.

But Miss Coates – the battleship, the dragon, the despiser of boys and anything small and cheeky, the anti-noise campaigner – was no coward. When her turn came she scrambled and squeezed and wriggled and slithered with the best of them. She emerged, with helping hands from Jayne and Toby, into the darkness of Ben's garden, and freedom.

Charles Blake was worried. It was most odd how his cousin had disappeared like that without saying a word. Frankly, he didn't know what to do about it. He thought of calling the police, but it was wasting their time if she'd just popped into a neighbour's and perhaps forgotten about him.

When he had finished his second drink he went upstairs calling "Edith!" in a loud voice that seemed silly when he knew in his heart he was alone in the house. He searched all the rooms again. Then he went downstairs calling "Edith!" in a loud voice in case she had come in while he was upstairs. He searched all the rooms down there. After that he spent another five minutes looking round the garden, not calling "Edith!" this time because he didn't want to disturb the neighbours. Then another five minutes trying to find if the house had a cellar (which it didn't). He finally spent ten minutes getting into the loft and searching that, all without success.

If she had popped into a neighbour's, he didn't know which one, and he certainly didn't want to create a hue and cry. It still wasn't eleven o'clock – the deadline for keeping his cousin "out of the way". He now had an uneasy feeling, though, that her disappearance was strongly connected with the children's doings, but he couldn't think what. Perhaps they had kidnapped her and hauled her up into the tree-house . . .

At ten o'clock Mr Blake poured himself another drink and sat down. At a quarter past ten he poured himself a fourth and checked all over the house again, but it somehow seemed slightly less urgent, more like a regular duty, or being on watch. At half past ten he was jolted from a pleasant little sleep by the sound of footsteps in the hall. He scrambled unsteadily to his feet as Miss Coates appeared quite unexpectedly in the sitting-room doorway. Mr Blake gasped and swayed at the strange apparition.

She looked like a scarecrow. Her beautiful pink cocktail dress was torn and smothered with mud; her white shoes were scraped and dirty; her hair looked as if it had been through a car wash with the sunroof open. Her face was filthy, and her glasses were lurking at a funny angle on her dusty nose. But through the murk of her appearance there shone a bright and sunny smile.

Mr Blake stared at her in horror. He'd had one drink too many and found that his lips didn't work properly at first.

"Where the bevil have you deen?" he stuttered. He felt there was something wrong about this, and added with great care, "I've mished you."

Miss Coates moved forward slightly, and bits of dirt and twigs bounced on to the carpet. She held up an old tin box.

Mr Blake, suddenly feeling much more sober, stared at it.

"I believe you wanted this," said his cousin.

Mr Blake stared and stared and stared. He reached out for the box, but Miss Coates gently pulled it away from his grasp.

"I – I can't understand what's going on," he said. "Can someone explain?" His drowsiness was beginning to disappear and he seemed to have regained control of his speech.

"Naitabals!" barked Miss Coates. It was a command.

"Naitabals?" began Mr Blake, then stopped. Five more

125

sets of feet were heard in the hall, and five more dirty faces appeared in the doorway behind Miss Coates.

Now Mr Blake stared at the Naitabals. Edith was smiling, and they were smiling as well. It was all a complete mystery. He didn't understand the last few hours at all.

"What — ?" he said.

"You," said Miss Coates, tucking the metal box firmly under her arm, "are going to make two strong coffees and five hot chocolate drinks, and *we* are going to get cleaned up."

Miss Coates and the Naitabals turned *en masse* and started towards the staircase.

"But what about the box?" spluttered Mr Blake.

"The box?" said Miss Coates, innocently.

"Aren't you going to give it to me?"

"No," said his cousin firmly. "You've earned a *look* at it by doing what you did so *badly* for the children. *You were supposed to keep me out of the way until eleven o'clock*. You failed. To earn a look *inside* the box, you'll have to do something for *me*, as well."

Mr Blake saw that argument was useless. He was a small pawn in a big chess game: he didn't even know how to play. No one seemed to want to tell him the rules, either. He heaved a very tired sigh and made his way carefully to the kitchen, holding on to the walls.

"A man's work is *never* done," he murmured.

When the Naitabals (and Miss Coates) were thoroughly washed and scrubbed, and the worst mud had dried and been brushed from their clothes and shoes, they returned to the sitting room and started to discuss their plans.

Mr Blake was sworn to secrecy and put out of his misery by being told the whole story. The others had discussed upstairs how much he ought to be told, but they had all agreed that Mr Blake (and his car) would be indispensable for what had to be done. The paintings had to be returned to their rightful owners, none of whom should know where they came from.

"Why don't we just post them all to the police and let them sort it out?" said Mr Blake, who somehow hadn't yet entered into the spirit of the thing. His suggestion was howled down by everyone (including Miss Coates) as being too easy and unexciting.

"What we want," said Miss Coates, who was bright-eyed and enjoying herself more than she had for years, "is as much publicity as possible for some *causes*. When these paintings are returned it will be *front page news*, and it would be *criminal* of us to miss such an opportunity. Now, there are five paintings and there are five Naitabals. I want each of you to tell me the name of a charity."

"Naitabals want to save the Earth," said Ben. "Mine is Friends of the Earth."

"Greenpeace," said Charlotte.

"Worldwide Fund for Nature," said Jayne.

Miss Coates looked at Boff and Toby.

"We've got to look after *people* as well," said Boff. "So I'll choose Oxfam."

"And I'll choose Cancer Research," said Toby.

"Excellent," said Miss Coates.

Then the discussion started. Ben's clever ideas for stopping Cedric Morgan telling anyone about the well were approved. A small working party was set up for the small hours when they were sure there would be no spying from the Naitabal hut. A day in London for Mr Blake was planned in full. Armed with what Miss Coates already knew, he would find out where the paintings came from, and obtain wigs, false noses, beards and moustaches, all without raising suspicions.

It was well past one o'clock in the morning when the Naitabals went to sleep on the sitting-room floor, exhausted and happy.

CHAPTER THIRTEEN

Onfessions-cang

Cedric Morgan sat up in bed and rubbed his eyes. He knew it was a wonderful day to wake up to, but for a few seconds he couldn't remember why. Then he realised, and with a whoop of joy sprang out of bed and threw on the first clothes that came to hand. It was eight o'clock. He had meant to get up earlier, but the night's adventures had left him tired. When he had eventually gone to bed he hadn't been able to sleep for ages thinking about Ben Tuffin and Toby and silly old Barry and Jayne and Charlotte. They'd all been locked in that underground place all night, and he hoped they were freezing cold.

Yes, it was the day when he was going round to see Miss Coates. He was going to *tell* her that Ben Tuffin and all his stupid friends had trespassed in her garden and were locked in that funny well of hers.

Cedric was very pleased with himself. His trick with the compliment slip and Mr Elliott's van had worked better than he dared hope. His importance in the eyes of his gang had risen considerably, and they were now the official residents of the magnificent tree-house in Mr Elliott's garden. Ben Tuffin and the *stupid* old others had spent a very bad night. They were going to be caught red-handed and land in big, big trouble. All he had to do was to get round to Miss Coates's house and tell her.

Cedric couldn't help smirking to himself. Several times he burst out laughing and giggling. It was going to be one

128

of the funniest and happiest days of his life.

When he was fully dressed, he went to wake Doris, who was buried under a heap of duvet and blankets.

At half past eight Miss Coates heard her front doorbell ring and went to answer it. On her doorstep stood four children. The one in front – obviously the Cedric Morgan of whom she had been told – was smirking ingratiatingly. The other three hung back at his rear, looking somewhat bewildered at the pace of events that had obviously over-taken them. All three had been woken up at an extraordi-narily early hour (for them) to be force-fed Cedric's news. It had been reluctantly agreed that half past eight was not too early to call.

"Can I help you?" said Miss Coates sternly. In her mind she was pleased that all their preparations for this event had been completed. After a good night's sleep she was back to her immaculate self, quite ready for what was to come. The Naitabals had been roused and despatched early so that they shouldn't be seen with Miss Coates. They didn't want to add any credibility to what Cedric had witnessed.

"My name is Cedric Morgan. This is my sister Doris, and these are my friends, Andy and Amanda."

"Yes? How do you do?"

"We *saw* something last night, and we thought we ought to tell you."

"Oh. Perhaps you'd better come in, then."

The four children, tidy because the day hadn't started yet, trooped in and sat in Miss Coates's comfortable chairs. Miss Coates disappeared and fetched Mr Blake, who had already told her that he wasn't going to miss this conversation for the world. Mr Blake stood next to his cousin.

"Now," said Miss Coates in a business-like voice, her

129

face still set and stern, "what is it that you saw?"

"I was in the tree-house, and—"

"Do you mean the *nice* tree-house over the back of my garden," interrupted Miss Coates, "or that *ramshackle* old thing two doors away?"

Cedric's fixed grin faded slightly at this backhanded insult. He tried to ignore his feelings, and continued stoically.

"The one that overlooks your garden—"

"But that one belongs to Ben Tuffin and his friends, surely?" interrupted Miss Coates again.

"N-no-o. At least, it *did*." Cedric brightened again as he realised that he could tell tales about Ben Tuffin's other activities. "But they were very naughty and crashed Mr Elliott's van on purpose—"

"They're too young to *drive*, surely?" interjected Miss Coates.

"No," said Cedric. The smile had all but disappeared again, and he was just beginning to feel irritated. "They played a *trick* on him and let the handbrake off, and the van rolled down the hill and went into a tree and" – seeing Miss Coates about to interrupt again, he quickened his pace – "Mr-Elliott-was-very-cross-and-threw-them-out-of-his-tree-house."

"That sounds a very dangerous thing for Mr Elliott to have done," protested Miss Coates. "That tree-house is very high up. He could have broken their legs, or even their necks."

"No-o," began Cedric, annoyed now. "I mean—"

This time it was Mr Blake's turn to interrupt. He had been quietly enjoying the spectacle of his lady cousin stalling the enemy, but now something in their story had made him suspicious.

"Did you say Mr Elliott's *van*?" he asked suddenly.

Cedric turned his attention to the new voice.

"Y-yes."

130

"When was this?"

"Y-yesterday. At dinner time."

"You mean in the evening?"

"No," – irritably – "One o'clock."

"Ah! Lunch time, then."

"Yes. *Lunch* time."

"But I saw *you* hanging around Mr Elliott's van when I came out of his house about that time."

"Me?" protested Cedric.

"Yes, you. You were stooping down by the front wheel fiddling with a piece of string and half a brick."

"N-not me," said Cedric.

"Oh – you deny it, do you?"

A great red sunset spread over Cedric Morgan's face and down to the distant horizon of his collar.

"I – I was just *playing*," he said, but his voice sounded weak and unconvincing.

"Is that what you came to tell us?" said Miss Coates sweetly. She turned to her cousin. "Isn't that nice, Charles? And I thought modern children were *deceitful*, *vulgar*, and *selfish*. Yet here we have an example of four children who realise that an *injustice* has been done, and have come to a *neutral* grown-up to confess. Of course, it would have been *too* much to expect them to go *direct* to Mr Elliott and confess because that would have demanded even *greater* courage."

There was a stunned silence from Cedric Morgan. Andy and Amanda, who were just starting to wake up, began to realise that Cedric's glowing account of how he was going to "fix" Ben Tuffin and his stupid gang was not going according to plan. Doris Morgan glared at her brother as if he was something the cat had sicked up.

"I'm an old friend of Eddie Elliott's as well," said Mr Blake cheerily. "I'll pop round later and tell him you've done the decent thing and confessed and ask him not to be too hard on you."

"That's marvellous!" said Miss Coates.

Cedric felt as if he had been given a nice box of chocolates and found it full of tarantulas. He stumbled on determinedly.

"But what we came to tell you, was—"

"Oh – something else, children? My word, it *is* confession time." Miss Coates became magnanimous in her brightness. "I know – I'll make it easier for you – you want to apologise for shooting those acorns into my garden yesterday morning, don't you? Well – that's all right – but don't do it again. Someone could get *blinded* you know."

Events had moved so quickly that Cedric was almost lost. He had come to report the single crime of somebody else. So far, he had somehow confessed to two of his own and was no further forward with his original plan. He was tired through lack of sleep as it was. Now he had the feeling that his brilliant run of luck was coming to an end. Doggedly, against all the odds, he continued his story.

"*I was in the tree-house*," he said firmly, "*late last night*, and I'd finished my comic and my lemonade and my sweets, and I discovered there were *peep*-holes in the side overlooking your garden. When I opened one up and looked through it I saw a *light* shining out of your *well*." Cedric had said all of this in one breath for fear of further interruption. He snatched another lungful of air, and ploughed on. "And then I saw most of Ben Tuffin's gang going down the well, and I went down out of the tree-house – which wasn't very quick 'cos it was dark an' I wasn't used to it – and I climbed the fence and ran through your rose bed and looked down the well and there was a *door*" – another deep breath – "and there was a key in it and I *locked them in* and they're *still there now* because *I've got the key*!"

He held up the key of the air-raid shelter. His smug grin had returned, and he was looking expectantly from Miss Coates to Mr Blake and back again. His grin began to slip away as he realised that neither grown-up was in the least impressed by his story. They didn't seem to be reacting in the way he had expected – in fact, they were looking at him as if he was *mad*.

"You others are very quiet about all this," said Mr Blake kindly. "Did any of *you* share this strange experience?"

The other three, looking like thunder at Cedric's back, shook their heads.

"He told us to come here," said Andy, mumbling. "It wasn't *our* idea."

Miss Coates gave a light little laugh, as if humouring their leader.

"Cedric," she began, slowly, "when you had finished your comic and your lemonade and your sweets, was it very late?"

"Quite late, Miss."

"Ah! Do you think you might have slept a little bit?"

Cedric was confused.

"Well – I – I might have. Just a *bit*. Why? What's that got to do with anything?"

Miss Coates heaved the sigh of one who is talking to the class dunce.

"Cedric – my well is a *dummy* well. It doesn't have a proper deep shaft like a proper well. It's just some bricks built to look like a well. The top of the well is filled with water and there are goldfish inside. You can't have looked down and seen a door, because there *isn't one*."

Cedric blinked.

"I'll show you," he said. "If we can go out in your garden, I'll show you!"

"Very well," said Miss Coates, patiently.

She led the way into the garden. Cedric marched confidently after her, followed by Doris, Andy and Amanda with murderous expressions on their faces. Mr Blake was thoroughly enjoying himself. His visit to his cousin was turning out to be much more interesting than he ever could have imagined.

They reached the well. Miss Coates stood back and beckoned them. The Igmopong stepped forward. The Igmopong looked into the well. They saw a dummy well with goldfish swimming around inside it.

"B-but it *was*!" said Cedric, lamely.

"Now, let's look at this logically," said Mr Blake, brightly, as if trying to be on Cedric's side. "You said you came across the rose bed, didn't you?"

"Yes!" A ray of hope. A straw for a drowning boy.

"Well, then. The soil has been damp these last days. Let's look in the rose bed. If this was late last night, your footprints will still be there, won't they?"

"Yes! They will!"

They all marched over to the rose bed. Cedric's mouth dropped open in despair. The rose bed was beautifully raked with not a hint of a footstep anywhere.

"I raked it yesterday after that naughty Ben Tuffin ran across it," said Miss Coates. "What funny *dreams* children have sometimes. *I* had some very funny dreams when I was your age. Once I dreamt—"

"But the *key*!" interrupted Cedric, quite rudely. "I took the *key*!" He held it up.

"Good heavens!" said Mr Blake, tapping his pockets. "My back door key! I wondered where I left it, and now I realise! It must have slipped out of my pocket when I was squatting in the tree-house yesterday!"

Without further ceremony, Mr Blake snatched the key from Cedric's greedy grasp and popped it into his own pocket. Cedric stared forlornly at his empty hand.

"That's another little mystery solved!" said Mr Blake, cheerfully. "I think these children deserve some refreshments, don't you, Edith?"

"I certainly do, Charles."

Mr Blake chuckled.

"You modern children amaze me! The stories you make up! All you had to do was bring me the key say 'Please, sir, we found this in the tree-house, and we've brought it back'!"

Mr Blake and Miss Coates laughed, but Cedric and his gang saw nothing funny in the situation at all.

"B-But they're still locked inside!" came Cedric's last desperate plea. "They'll *starve*!"

"Who?" said Miss Coates, raising her voice deliberately. "*Ben Tuffin*? Why, *I can hear him in his garden right now*!"

Right on cue, Ben Tuffin's lusty voice was suddenly heard beyond the thick trees and hedges: "Hi, Charlotte!" It was followed by the answering call from Charlotte lagoon: "Hi, Ben!"

The destruction of Cedric's mission was complete.

CHAPTER FOURTEEN

Attle-bang

With Mr Blake rushing off to London to carry out his research, there was no time for him to catch Mr Elliott at home in the morning. Instead, Mr Blake wrote a note to Mr Elliott. It explained how the damage to his van and house window had occurred, and asked him to reconsider the Naitabals' ban from the tree-house. But as Mr Elliott had already left for work when the note was delivered, his decision wouldn't be known until lunch time. As a result, a strange calm settled over the Naitabal domain for the rest of the morning.

The Igmopong, realising that they had a breathing space, started preparing for the battle that would inevitably ensue as soon as Mr Elliott was informed.

"Well!" Doris exploded, when they had finally left Miss Coates's house. "A nice mess you made of that! Fancy tellin' 'em it was you what messed up Mr Elliott's van!"

"I didn't *tell* 'em. They knew. That Mr Break or whatever-his-name-was said he *saw* me."

"And *did* he?"

"I dunno. I didn't think anyone saw me. But he knew about the string and the bit of brick, and me wedging the front wheel, so he must have done. He couldn't have known about *those* unless he saw them."

Doris shrugged.

"Huh! All I know is you've just made a proper mess of

136

everything just when we were *gettin'* somewhere. As soon as Mr Elliott finds out, you're for it."

"*I'm* for it? You *helped* me."

"It was your idea, not ours."

Andy and Amanda said "Yeah!" half-heartedly, not quite sure which side to take until the argument developed further.

"As soon as old Elliott finds out," Doris went on, rubbing it in, "we'll be out of here in no time. We'll be back in *that* thing, over there."

"No we won't," said Cedric aggressively. "If old Ben Tuffin and that stupid gang want their tree-house back, they'll have to *fight* for it."

In spite of their disappointment over losing their new tree-house after such a short stay, the idea of a fight for it began to take on an exciting appeal.

"They wouldn't *smash* their way in," said Amanda. "That'd mean spoiling their own place, and it's too nice to do that to it."

"They can't get in through the roof. We can use the padlock on the inside to stop them getting in there."

"Let's lock it now," suggested Andy.

They clambered up, fixed the padlock to the two staples and clicked it shut.

"There! And they can't get in through the trap-door in the floor because *that's* bolted on the inside. Even if they had a ladder they couldn't get in."

"And all the windows lock from the inside. They can't get in *those*."

"They could *starve* us out," said Amanda.

"We'll need lots of food – and drinks."

"We'll need more torches and batteries."

"We'll need paper and pencil for messages."

"We'll need weapons."

"Catapults."

"Bags of flour."

"Bows and arrows."

"Acorns."

"Mud pies."

"Water-bombs."

Doris smiled smugly.

"I don't see how they can get *us* out. They won't know what's hit 'em."

"We could never get *them* out," said Andy.

"Exactly. So they won't get *us* out."

"They'll try a lot harder because it *belongs* to them," said Amanda.

Everyone agreed that they would need to prepare for a long siege. They would ask their parents' permission to sleep several nights if necessary. They set out two by two to collect their materials and visit the bathroom, leaving two behind to guard the fort and keep it locked.

In the meantime, the Naitabals had not been idle. They were holding a war cabinet in Boff's bedroom, overlooking Boff Island and the Sea of Debris next door. From there, they could just see the vague shadows of their enemies arguing inside the Naitabal hut.

"We could *flush* 'em out," said Charlotte, wickedly. "Stick the end of a hosepipe through one of the peepholes an' *soak* 'em."

"We could *smoke* 'em out," said Jayne, not to be out-done. "We could light a bonfire and send the smoke up a tube into all the holes."

"Or just light the bonfire underneath 'em," said Toby. "*Burn* 'em out."

"The trouble is," said Boff, more seriously, "whatever clever ideas we use for getting them out, *they* can use against us in the future. Soaking them sounds possible, but it would spoil the inside of the hut for a while – and give the Igmopong ideas. We'd only have them giving us a soaking sometime."

"I agree," said Ben. "They've never had many ideas of their own – and we don't want to give them any now."

"What other ways are there?" said Toby. "The girls' ones are the best so far."

"A straightforward attack is no good," said Charlotte. "They've got the advantage. If any of us go anywhere near, we'll get fired at from all directions."

There was a short silence while everyone thought.

"We could *starve* them out," said Toby at last, not very seriously. "Trouble is, it would take about three weeks, and we can't wait that long."

"What we need is a secret weapon," said Ben. "A weapon *they* haven't got, so they can't use it on us."

"There is a weak spot . . . " said Boff, slowly.

All heads turned to Boff. They were used to Boff coming up with the occasional brilliant idea, and hoped this was going to be one of them.

"Well?" they said.

Boff was still thinking.

"How many of those black plastic bags have we got in *Roject-pong Ubmarine-song*?" he said.

"Lots," said Ben. "Twenty or thirty, maybe."

"Good." Boff smiled. "Anyone got any Sellotape?"

"Hooray! Boff's got an idea!" said Charlotte.

"I've got some," said Jayne. "A big roll."

"It's only half the idea," said Boff. "We still need a secret weapon."

"What's the half idea? Tell us that and we might be able to come up with a secret weapon to fit."

But before Boff could tell them anything, Jayne, who was on look-out near Boff's window, suddenly hissed with excitement.

"Look!" she said. They stopped talking and looked.

139

"Mr Elliott's going down the Sea of Debris towards the Naitabal hut!"

Within seconds they were all at the window. Sure enough, Mr Elliott was making his way briskly down his garden. Clouds of cement and plaster dust flew off his overalls and boots with each step. He stood beneath the tree-house and looked up at the occupants.

"We can't hear what he's saying!"

"Quick, Boff, open your window!"

"Sorry," said Boff. "This window doesn't open. It's nailed up."

"Oh, no!"

In a way, they didn't need to hear what Mr Elliott was saying. It was obvious from the way he was standing, and from the gestures he was making with his arms, exactly what he was saying. The Igmopong's pale faces had now appeared at the window of the Naitabal hut. Conversation, however, appeared to be rather one-sided. Mr Elliott's finger was shaking at them, then pointing towards Cedric Morgan's garden, then shaking at them again.

If only Boff's window could be opened! There was no time to run outside in case they missed some of the action.

Suddenly the mood of the Igmopong seemed to change from innocent protestation to belligerent defiance. They had obviously answered back. Now Mr Elliott's finger was shaking at them more violently (still emitting baby puffs of dust), and more words were being said. Then a surprising thing happened. Mr Elliott had moved right under the side of the Naitabal hut to get his point across, when suddenly a white blob of something fell from the window. It happened so quickly that Mr Elliott scarcely had time to duck. The object burst, and his head and body were enveloped in an exploding white blizzard.

"I don't believe it!" said Boff. "They've dropped a flour bomb on him!"

Ben could no longer stand not being able to hear anything. He disappeared downstairs and into the garden to listen behind the fence. The others watched as Mr Elliott, far from exploding in anger, simply walked back up the path, now giving off slightly more clouds of dust than usual.

Charlotte and Jayne were shrieking with laughter, and Toby and Boff were just awestruck at the Igmopong's stupidity.

"Poor Mr Elliott hardly looks any different to normal with a whole bag of flour on his head!" Charlotte laughed.

Then Ben came back upstairs to report Cedric's parting words, shouted at Mr Elliott's retreating figure, "I'm *so* sorry, Mr Elliott, it *slipped*!"

The Naitabals were delighted. Dropping a flour bomb on Mr Elliott in his own garden while trespassing in his tree-house was not going to help the Igmopong.

Then Boff's doorbell rang.

"Mr Elliott!" said Boff. "Come on!"

They all rushed down the stairs. Boff opened the door to reveal Mr Elliott, looking even whiter than usual, standing on the doorstep.

"Now don't ask me in," he said. "I'm a bit dusty."

The Naitabals stared.

"I've come to apologise, kids," Mr Elliott continued. "I've been told by a friend it wasn't you lot who smashed my van. I'm sorry, and you can have the tree-house back. I know who did it for definite, so don't you worry."

"Thank you, Mr Elliott!"

"That's wonderful, Mr Elliott!"

"I've told them they must be out by eight o'clock tomorrow morning," said Mr Elliott. Then he winked – a pink wink in a sea of white. "That means you can ambush them when they come out, doesn't it?"

"Wow! Yes it does!" shouted the Naitabals.

"Of course," said Mr Elliott, turning to go, "I won't complain to their parents until after eight o'clock tomorrow, so if they haven't left by then" – he raised his eyebrows good-humouredly – "I'm afraid you'll have to find some way of getting them out yourselves."

"We'll do it with pleasure!"

Mr Elliott smiled briefly through his coating of flour and departed without further fuss. The Naitabals gathered once more in Boff's room to finalise their plans.

"Well," said Ben, grinning like the others, "what was your plan for getting them out, Boff?"

"Yes," said Jayne. "Tell us and maybe we'll think of a secret weapon!"

Briefly, Boff told them how they could break through the weak point in the tree-house defences. Their faces lit up.

"That's wonderful, Boff!"

"Brilliant!"

Then, suddenly, it was Charlotte's turn to be brilliant. She was so surprised with her own idea that she suddenly stood up and shouted.

"*We have got a secret weapon!*" she exploded.

At six o'clock the following morning the Igmopong were still tightly packed together after an uneasy night, made worse because three of them were afraid of the dark. Sleeping space was limited because no one had dared to sleep on the trap-door in case it mysteriously fell open during the night. Instead, they had piled it with provisions and weapons, hoping to make it more secure against attack from below. At one o'clock in the morning their slumber had been disturbed by mysterious bangings from below. Andy had convinced everyone it was a ghost, and they had all been too scared to leave the safety of their sleeping bags to investigate.

At one minute past six they were rudely awakened by something thudding into the side of the hut.

"What was that?" said Andy.

"If you'd get your big feet off my chest I could see what it was," said Cedric, struggling to get upright.

Amanda was nearest the window and had managed to stretch herself to look out.

"Ben Tuffin, creeping away to the west, bow in hand," she announced.

"Must be a message on an arrow," said Cedric, yawning. "See what it says, Andy."

"What, me? How do I know where it is?"

"Look for it, stupid."

There was a short argument over responsibilities and leadership, at the end of which the west window was opened very gingerly by Andy. The arrow was discovered within easy reach of the opening. He retrieved it, closed the window, and unfolded the message, which was written in bright red magic marker pen.

"It's a *poem*!" said Doris contemptuously.

It read:

> We are the Naitabals
> You are the Igmopong
> We are right
> You are wrong.
>
> We are the Naitabals
> You are the Igmopong
> Leave this tree
> You don't belong
>
> We are the Naitabals
> You are the Igmopong
> You will die
> When you hear our song.

143

"Pooh! Rubbish!" spat Cedric. "I could write a better one than that!"

"Go on, then," said Doris. "Write one."

"Well, I'm not going to write one *now*, am I!"

"Yes, you are. They want a reply."

There followed another argument concerning leadership and responsibilities, at the end of which Cedric said, "All right, then, I will!"

There was a short silence while Cedric put pencil to paper. At the end of a session of grunts, erasures, and "Ah, yeses!", the poem was held up for approval. Doris was impressed, despite herself. It read:

You are the ones who pong
And we don't care if you sing your silly song.
We're here to stay
Not just for today
If you want to shift us, you'll have to get King Kong.

Everyone sniggered and thought it hugely funny.

"All right," said Doris. "Send it."

They opened up the north window carefully. Cedric wrapped the poem round an arrow with an elastic band to hold it in place. For once his aim was good, and the arrow flew through the air and clung precariously to the bark of Boff's big tree. A shadowy figure darted out, collected the message, and disappeared again.

Five minutes later another arrow thudded into the side of the Naitabal hut. The message said simply:

Battle commences at eight o'clock.

The first hint that the Igmopong received of the opening of hostilities was at exactly eight o'clock. Low, yet clear and piercing, the sound of chanting voices suddenly floated through the still morning air like a swan song, slow and mournful:

> *E-thong Aitabal-ning Ree-tong,*
> *Preads-song Its-ing Ranches-bang,*
> *Over-ong Ose-thong O-whung,*
> *Eserve-dang O-tong E-bang Ere-thong.*

Then there was a deathly silence.

"What did the song say?" whispered Andy.

"How are we supposed to know that, stupid?" said Doris. "It's just some silly song they were talking about in their poem."

Andy's face went suddenly white.

"They said after the song, we die!"

"Oh, shut up!" whispered Cedric. "And why are we whispering?"

Before Doris could screw her face up nastily enough to answer, the chant began again, as mysterious and unnerving as before. They didn't know what it meant, but the Igmopong, crouched now beneath the windows, listened closely to every syllable, as if trying to understand its meaning:

> *Only-ong E-thong Ood-geng,*
> *O-whung Ook-ling after-ang,*
> *E-thong Earth-eng,*
> *All-shong Eep-king It-ing.*

A few seconds after the chanting subsided, the four heads of the Igmopong rose to look out of two of the windows.

"Can you see anyone?"

"No."

"What are they doing, then?"

"How am I supposed to know? I'm not one of them, am I?"

"Do you think we're really going to die?" said Andy, still white.

No one bothered to answer.

"They can't touch us. We're safe up here," said Amanda suddenly.

There was a long pause, then Cedric said nervously, "How about getting our weapons ready?"

"They are ready," snapped Doris. "All we've got to do is pick 'em up an' throw 'em at the enemy. The only problem at the moment is that we can't see any enemy."

While the Igmopong were distracted, Ben Tuffin and Boff climbed the long branch from Boff Island, then stood on top of the Naitabal hut listening to the voices inside.

They carefully placed the rolled-up black plastic parcels on the sloping roof. From Ben's back pocket projected a large screwdriver, and from Boff's, a hammer. Together they held up the first of the long packages and waited for the second diversion – the appearance of Jayne and Charlotte. They were in Naitabal battledress, dragging a hosepipe and armed with catapults and Naitabal acorns, heading for the west window. As acorns began to rain on the wooden west wall, accompanied by the jeers of the Igmopong who were safely inside, so Ben tapped nails along the edge of the black plastic sheet on the north side of the roof.

"There's someone on the roof!" shouted Doris and Amanda together.

"They can't get in!" sneered Cedric. "It's locked!"

A few moments later there was a partial eclipse as Ben and Boff unrolled the black plastic bags that were taped together and strengthened, and dropped the huge sheet over the north side, completely obscuring the window.

146

"What are they doing?" screamed Doris.

A few more nails tapped in made it impossible for the Igmopong to open the north window (even if they'd thought of it). Then Ben and Boff were unrolling and fixing the second and third sheets to cover up the west and south sides. Within five minutes the Igmopong were blind – they couldn't see out of any windows. The only view available was through the peep-holes overlooking Miss Coates's garden, which were no use to them at all.

"They still can't touch us!" argued Cedric, pathetically. "The trap-door's shut and bolted and the roof's padlocked on the *in*side."

Within seconds, Boff was running back along the branch to fetch the ropes to re-make his bridge. Ben was kneeling by the trap-door on the roof unscrewing the hinges. By the time Boff returned and hooked up the rope on its stays again, Ben was ready.

Then Boff went back along the rope bridge to where Toby waited with their secret weapon.

"Well!" said Doris, accusingly. "A fat lot of use *flour-bombs* are now! I suppose we're supposed to chuck 'em *up* through the *roof* or something so they fall back down on us! Whose stupid idea were they in the first place?"

"Yours!" said everyone, and Doris shut up.

The four of them were half crouched in the dim twilight of the hut. They had opened the peep-holes on Miss Coates's side to let in as much light as possible, and some pencils of light stood up from the holes and cracks in the floor. The whole effect gave them lined and mottled faces that made their apprehension more tangible.

"What do we do now?" hissed Cedric.

"You're the leader," hissed back Doris. "You tell us!"

"Well, they still can't get in."

"Perhaps they're going to *gas* us!" said Andy.

"Don't be stupid! That'd be *murder*. They can't go round *murd'rin'* people."

"What're they gonna *do*, then?" whispered Amanda.

Only a few seconds later, they found out. Suddenly, inexplicably, the trap-door in the roof opened outwards. Its padlock was still attached on one side, and its loose hinges were flapping on the other. The hut was flooded with blinding light. The Igmopong, ready with their weapons, blinked and adjusted their eyes to the scene above them.

On the edge of the hole, supported on either side by Boff and Toby, stood the Naitabals' secret weapon. The Igmopong stood transfixed, the weapons in their hands dropping down towards the floor.

"Open the trap-door!" screamed Doris. "Let's get out of here!"

The Igmopong frantically struggled with the bolts and the rope ladder to get out as fast as they could. The secret weapon was lowered gently down through the hole in the roof, its stick swishing, and its jam jar gyrating in a vicious circle.

The ambush was complete. The Igmopong half fell down the rope ladder in their desperate attempt to escape the secret weapon. At the bottom they found themselves penned in by tall stakes and chicken wire, erected during the small hours of darkness. Almost before they knew what was happening, the rope ladder had been pulled up into the Naitabal hut. They were trapped.

First, a bag of flour dropped through the trap-door hit Cedric Morgan on the head and burst like a waterfall in a plume of spray.

"I'm *so* sorry, Cedric, it *slipped*!" mimicked a voice from above in Cedric's slimy tones.

Then Doris Morgan shouted something rude and made

the mistake of looking up to see where the bag had come from. She found out as the second one landed on her upturned face. Then Andy and Amanda were coated as they tried unsuccessfully to scramble through the wire that hemmed them in.

"Oh, dear!" shouted Charlotte and Jayne sarcastically, "those naughty boys have made your clothes all messy! We'll have to clean you up!"

Without further delay the hosepipe was trained on the four squirming figures in the pen. The stream of water soaked their clothes, their faces, and even inside their mouths as they tried to scream or shout abuse. And as the deluge continued, voices above them were saying:

"You'd better take your other things with you, Cedric!"

"Here they are!"

And the Igmopong were hit with all the flour bombs, acorns, mud pies and water-bombs that they had stored up for use against the Naitabals. Alternately encrusted with flour, pelted with missiles and washed and re-washed with the hosepipe, the Igmopong received their just reward.

At the top of the Sea of Debris, Mr Elliott was laughing as he hadn't laughed in years.

CHAPTER FIFTEEN

Unburglars

The Naitabals breakfasted on Igmopong lemonade and Igmopong macaroons. For his courage, Harry was officially enrolled as an honorary sub-Naitabal (or an Onnermy Sum-Baitabal as Harry preferred to call himself), and at half past eight the gathering was called to a close. After promising never to hit anyone with his jam jar except in self-defence, Harry was helped down the rope ladder.

"It was only a *game*, Harry," Charlotte had told him sternly, "and you can't come to Naitabal meetings except special ones."

"Can Onnermy Sum-Baitabals come to special ones?" said Harry.

"Yes, they can."

Harry departed, satisfied. The remaining Naitabals then set about putting the hut back to its former glory. They graciously returned everything that belonged to the Igmopong (except the lemonade and macaroons), and made everything secure. They would worry about the weakness in its defences another day.

At nine o'clock they assembled in Miss Coates's sitting room, as arranged, to hear Mr Blake's report of his visit to London the day before. Then they discussed his plans for the unburgling of the five priceless paintings stolen by Miss Coates's father so many years before.

At one o'clock the meeting ended. The plans were set.

The Naitabals returned to their respective homes, exhilarated and deep in thought.

The following day Mr Blake, with the Naitabals' parents' permission, took them all to London for a "day out."

It was a day out that they would all remember for the rest of their lives. It was a day out that they would never be able to discuss with anyone else, except – the Naitabals.

As Miss Coates had predicted, the newspapers had plenty to say about the Naitabals' day in London – only, of course, there wasn't a single mention of the Naitabals. Most newspapers had something on the front page, with more details inside.

The Naitabals and their grown-up partners in uncrime spent a busy half hour buying all the different newspapers they could find and hiding them in the Naitabal hut for detailed consumption later.

The Times' headline was "Priceless Paintings Returned", while the *Observer*'s said "Fifty-year Art Mystery Solved". Other papers had "Charity Art Bonanza", "The Mysterious Appearing Paintings", "Borrowed Art Returned After Fifty Years", down to "Charity Art Scoop", "Art Thieves Cough Up", "Arty Charity Party", and "Charity Kids Anonymous".

The Naitabals knew that they could only show a secret interest in the articles, but Ben was lucky when his father drew attention to it over breakfast that morning.

"Well, what do you think of that?" said Mr Tuffin to his wife.

Mrs Tuffin, who was being Barbra Streisand at that moment, singing "People who eat treac-le, are the *stick*iest people in the wo-orld," but having difficulty with some of the high notes, stopped singing and listened to

151

what her husband was reading from the morning newspaper.

"Five Old Master paintings, stolen nearly fifty years ago, have suddenly reappeared in circumstances as mysterious as their original disappearance during the years of the Second World War.

"Monet's 'Harvest' taken from Park Grange during an air raid on 15 June 1941, was returned in an ordinary cardboard tube sent by registered post from London on Wednesday. Mrs Segrave, who was only fourteen years old when the painting disappeared from her father's estate said 'When I opened it I realised straight away what it was, but thought it was a hoax – someone sending me a copy. I called in an art expert immediately, and he has confirmed that it is the original. I am overjoyed. The painting was uninsured during the war, and its return is a wonderful surprise. I don't know where it's been for the last fifty years, but it's been well looked after.' A crudely written note returned with the painting politely asks for £10,000 to be donated to Friends of the Earth as a reward. Mrs Segrave has agreed to the payment. The note, with letters made up from native spears leaning against each other, is thought to be the work of some kind of cult.

"In a bizarre episode, the second painting, by Rubens, was discovered when Reginald Hooper re-opened his art gallery in Bond Street this morning. Spotlights had been altered to shine on this new addition to his stock in the back of the shop, and a note, similar to the one found at Park Grange, asked for a donation of £10,000 to be forwarded to Greenpeace. The back door of the shop was found to be open, as if someone had secreted themselves inside the shop during the afternoon and let themselves out when the replacement was accomplished. A witness thought that he had seen an old lady with white hair hanging around during the late afternoon, but couldn't be sure, and was unable to give any helpful description.

"The third painting was discovered in a garden shed, following a tip-off to the police. Charity: The Worldwide Fund for Nature. This was a Picasso which had disappeared from an auction room (now closed) in 1943.

"It seems that children were involved in the last two returns. In the fourth incident, a child in a bright red wig, with bright red horn-rimmed spectacles, and dressed in a bright red jumper, simply handed a rolled-up parcel to the enquiries desk at the British Museum, and asked the attendant there to give it to the 'boss'. On being questioned further, the child ran away. The rolled-up parcel contained a long lost picture by Renoir, 'Flowers in the Stream'. The cost? £10,000 to Cancer Research.

"The fifth painting, Turner's 'Romney Marsh' was left on a chair in the long room at Audley End, out of the reach of visitors. An attendant remembered admonishing two children she found behind the public barrier, but as they were carrying nothing, she knew that nothing had been taken. The picture was discovered later by cleaners. One child was very small and was wearing a Groucho face mask with a cigar. The other was wearing a full beard and dark glasses, and walked with a limp. The attendant thought they were 'mucking about' and didn't bother to pry further as they were so young, aged about eleven. The reward demanded in this case, again written in spears, was £10,000 to Oxfam.

"Commenting on the 'un-burglaries', a police spokesman said it was the strangest case of returned goods that had ever been known. There was no doubt that they came from a single source – perhaps a repentant burglar or millionaire. What mattered most was that the paintings were back, unharmed, where they belonged.

"He added that it would take months for the current owners to be identified, after taking into account insurance claims, deaths and estate duties.

"Asked if he thought the identity of the un-burglars

153

would ever be discovered, the police spokesman said 'he thought not'."

"Isn't that incredible?" said Mr Tuffin.

"S'wonderful," said Mrs Tuffin. "S'marvellous."

Mr Tuffin, suspecting the onset of another song, said: "How nice it must be to have kids with that kind of initiative."

Ben smiled and slipped outside with his hands over his ears as his mother started being Nat King Cole.

It was raining. In the chicken run a few brave chickens were pecking at the muddy soil, unaware of the part they had played in the adventure.

The irregular pattern of rain drops falling from the oak leaves beat a tattoo on the roof of the Naitabal hut. Inside, dry and warm and (almost) comfortable, seven people sat in as near a circle as was possible in the confined space. The five Naitabals, Ben, Boff, Charlotte, Jayne and Toby were there. So was Mr Blake, and so was Miss Coates, looking quite different in the pair of jeans she had insisted on wearing for her inaugural climb up the rope ladder.

In the middle of the rough circle was the metal box on which Mr Blake's fortunes depended. Next to Mr Blake was a large bag of tools and keys. In one corner was a pile of the day's newspapers.

"Well," said Miss Coates. "I think your tree-house is wonderful – far, far better than the one we used to have – and I think you're very lucky children."

They had already shown her its facilities and (some of) its secrets, including the holes they had used to spy on her own garden.

"I think I'd almost rather you had a window," she had murmured. "At least then I could *see* when you're spying on me."

154

They showed the grown-ups the escape hatch in the roof and explained how Boff padlocked it on the outside at night and used the rope bridge to get back to his own garden. And they explained some of their new security measures for preventing the Igmopong, or anyone else, getting in too easily.

"Can't they unscrew the hinges, as you did?" asked Mr Blake respectfully.

"No," said Ben. "We've put in screws that you can screw in, but you can't screw out again."

"Ingenious," murmured Miss Coates. She was beginning to feel glad that these formidable children were on her side after all, and not her enemies.

She coughed.

"Before Mr Blake opens the box," she said, in her best speech-making voice, "I would like to make an announcement."

There was an immediate silence, except for the rain drops and Ben whispering "Pigmo *atch-wung!*"

"I no longer have any use for my 'picture store' – I daren't call it anything else in case someone overhears – and I hereby give the Naitabals free use and access to it for ever."

"Hooray!" the cheer went up.

"*Thank you*, Miss Coates."

"We'll clean it up, Miss Coates."

"We'll have a *tea*-party in it, Miss Coates."

"*On condition*," said Miss Coates, raising her voice above the general tumult, "that its secret is kept for ever—"

"Hooray!"

"That means we'll always have to use *Roject-pong Ubmarine-song!*"

" – and – that you install proper safety alarms in case you are ever trapped—"

"*YES*, Miss Coates!"

155

"*Tunnels and underground places*," hissed Miss Coates, dropping her voice to an insistent whisper, "are *very dangerous*, and should *never* be constructed without adult supervision."

"No, Miss Coates."

"*So* – Mr Elliott must check its safety every three months."

"Yes, Miss Coates."

"*Thank you*, Miss Coates."

Mr Blake, who had masterminded the return of the stolen paintings, was joining in the celebrations whole-heartedly. But his eyes and hands wandered more and more towards the metal box that stood on the floor between them.

"Er – may we attempt to open the box now?" he said, nervously. His whole future would be decided on the contents of this box, and he wasn't sure he could stand the suspense any longer.

Miss Coates's white head rotated like a lighthouse beam as she addressed the Naitabals.

"Do you think Mr Blake has kept his part of the bargain?" she teased him.

"*Yes!*" said the Naitabals.

"Do you think he deserves to open the box?"

"*YES!*"

Turning to Mr Blake: "Well, you'd better open it, then, Charles – if you can."

But Mr Blake had come prepared. Knowing that the Naitabals had been unable to open its lock, he had brought along his precious bag of tools from the car. From it he took a large bunch of keys and a hacksaw.

"If the keys are no good," he said, "I'll saw the thing in half."

One by one he tried the keys. One by one they failed. Twenty keys, thirty keys, all the keys he had found in junk shops in his spare moments in London thinking about the box. Forty keys, all failed. His disappointment, and that of everyone else, was tangible as the sweat began to stand out in little beads on his shining forehead. He tried the last one, fingers shaking.

"No good," he said.

"There was a sudden jangle of more keys as Miss Coates leaned towards him and dangled another bunch.

"These are all the old keys I could find in the house," she said. "See if any of them are any good."

Eagerly, Mr Blake took them and tried key after key while everyone watched breathless with excitement. Some wouldn't fit in the lock at all; others went in and refused to turn; some went in and turned round, but did nothing, or got stuck half way. At last, a key went sweetly in the lock. Mr Blake's anxious fingers increased the pressure. There was a rusty-ish sort of click, and the lock yielded at last.

"*Yes!*" shouted the Naitabals.

Nervously, Mr Blake's hands held both sides of the metal lid and raised it up. His eyes, bulging with expectation, suddenly changed to disappointment and shock. The box fell from his hands on to the floor in the centre. All the others looked inside.

It was empty.

"Empty!" exclaimed Mr Blake. "All this – and empty!"

The Naitabals stared at the box that lay on the floor, fallen sideways, its lid gaping like the mouth of a gasping fish.

"Who'd want to bury an empty box?" said Charlotte, only speaking because it helped her to hold back a tear.

"What a shame!" said Jayne, with a catch in her voice.

Mr Blake looked up. His face was a mask of defeat. His business would crash after all. He would face the awful process of bankruptcy, of losing his house and just about everything he'd worked for . . .

But as he looked at Miss Coates there was suddenly a glimmer. It was the faint, unmistakable trace of wickedness that he had known in her as a ten year old. And he had seen it in this very tree over half a century before. She was smiling.

"You don't think for *one moment*," said Miss Coates deliberately, "that I could *stand* having that box in my house for a *whole day* while you were in London and *not open it*, do you?"

"You mean—?" Mr Blake was wrenched between hope and despair.

"Of course I mean. I tried all the keys in the house and couldn't get the silly thing open—"

"But that one opened it—" began Mr Blake, confused.

"*Of course it did*. That's because I took the whole thing down to the locksmith in the afternoon. He opened it in three minutes, and then made me that little key to fit . . ."

"You mean—?"

"Stop saying 'You mean' all the time, Charles. You're beginning to sound like a parrot."

There was a burst of laughter from the Naitabals.

"What I *mean*," said Miss Coates firmly, drawing out a sheaf of old-looking legal documents and thrusting them with a flourish under Mr Blake's nose, "is that *these papers* are what you've been looking for."

Mr Blake grabbed them like one possessed. He checked them. Sure enough, they were the valuable bonds and share certificates he had been told about. They were worth thousands of pounds and would be sufficient to pay his debts and rescue his business. He held them up and kissed them.

Then he kissed Miss Coates against her will and called her a wicked old devil, and the Naitabals shouted "*Ooray-heng!*" as one voice.

"Cock-a-doodle-oo!" said the cockerel.

David Schutte
Wake Up, It's Midnight!

Suddenly they heard a ghostly sound. It was the tapping of a typewriter, hanging in the dark air, haunting them . . .

The Naitabals have been asked to keep an eye on some valuable old furniture which belonged to Mrs Vormann – their mysterious neighbour who has just died. What could be simpler, they think.

But someone else is interested in the furniture too, especially the old lady's unusual and ornate desk. Whose are the footsteps that prowl the lonely house by night – and who will stop at nothing to discover its secrets?